At the door of the bedroom, Dane stopped in his tracks

On his bed lay Suzy, her two little angels sleeping soundly beside her…drawing him in with their cherubic faces. Tingles ran over his arms. He allowed himself to give Suzy a thorough once-over.

What the hell was she doing in his room? On his bed?

Dane intended to tell Goldilocks when she awakened that his bed was not "just right" for her.

No. He couldn't do that. There were three of her family and only one of him.

Dane realized no matter how he fought it, staying at the Morgan ranch for a year with Suzy Winterstone and her girls was not going to be his easiest assignment.

Dear Reader,

I love writing about home, hearth and family. The older my children get, the more home means to me. So I was delighted to be able to write THE MORGAN MEN series, which started with *Texas Lullaby* (June 2008) and now continues with *The Texas Ranger's Twins*. Two more books follow—*The Secret Agent's Surprises* (February 2009) and *The Triplets' Rodeo Man* (March 2009). These are the stories of four brothers who learn that it's never too late to go home again.

The Morgan men are estranged from a father they haven't spoken to in years. But the elder Mr. Morgan is particularly clever at luring his boys home—with the promise of an inheritance, and the hope they'll become family men. Forgiveness is something the Morgan brothers will need to learn—and that's never an easy lesson! What a wonderful gift it is to discover that forgiveness is possible, and the light of home is always burning.

The Texas Ranger's Twins also kicks off a year-long celebration of heroes called MEN MADE IN AMERICA. Look for one book a month in 2009 that celebrates a hunky American male and his chosen profession!

Enjoy THE MORGAN MEN and MEN MADE IN AMERICA. See you next month!

Best wishes and much love,

Tina Leonard

Tina Leonard

THE TEXAS
RANGER'S TWINS

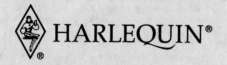

HARLEQUIN®

TORONTO • NEW YORK • LONDON
AMSTERDAM • PARIS • SYDNEY • HAMBURG
STOCKHOLM • ATHENS • TOKYO • MILAN • MADRID
PRAGUE • WARSAW • BUDAPEST • AUCKLAND

ISBN-13: 978-0-373-75245-4
ISBN-10:   0-373-75245-8

THE TEXAS RANGER'S TWINS

www.eHarlequin.com

Printed in U.S.A.

ABOUT THE AUTHOR

Tina Leonard is the bestselling author of over forty projects, including a popular thirteen-book miniseries for Harlequin American Romance. Her books have made the Waldenbooks, Ingram's, and Nielsen Bookscan bestseller lists. Tina feels she has been blessed with a fertile imagination and quick typing skills, excellent editors, and a family who loves her career. Born on a military base, she lived in many states before eventually marrying the boy who did her crayon printing for her in the first grade. Tina believes happy endings are a wonderful part of a good life. You can visit her at www.tinaleonard.com.

Books by Tina Leonard

Many thanks to my family,
who have always made my home a wonderful place

Chapter One

"Spare the rod, spoil the child"
—Josiah Morgan on his parenting philosophy
of raising four boys on his own

Suzy Winterstone didn't like the Morgan ranch. It was too big, too isolated and very scary at night. She walked inside the house, feeling chills that weren't from the January wind. The front door actually creaked when someone opened it, just like in an old movie. She told herself the hinges were cold and hadn't been used recently, but then she remembered Josiah Morgan had told her he had a farmhand who kept an eye on the property. So the hinges weren't unused—they were simply spooky.

All of five-foot-five and weighing about a hundred and thirty pounds, Suzy wasn't prepared to grapple with ghosts. According to Josiah's letter, a live-in house-keeper was badly needed at the ranch. She needed a job, and she dreamed of employment that would allow her to watch over her children. Here was a golden opportunity to achieve her heart's desire. Josiah Morgan said she'd be doing him a favor—he'd been very generous to her in the past and this job offer was no exception. Upon hearing that her boyfriend of three years had ended their relationship and had taken off for parts unknown, leaving her high and dry with twin babies, Josiah had set up a trust fund for the girls' college expenses. She'd felt very fortunate, but Mr. Morgan was known for his generous acts in the town of Union Junction. Some people said the old man was crazy, but most people thought he was kind and grandfatherly, including Suzy.

Suzy had been working as a nurse at the hospital up until her maternity leave and was fortunate to have insurance. She could always go back to nursing, but creaking doors aside, this would be a wonderful place to work for one year. Josiah wanted it kept clean, and he wanted it decorated for every holiday, as if a family lived there. Knowing she had sewing skills, he wanted new drapes made for the house, for which he'd pay her extra. The fabrics he'd chosen were stored somewhere in this cavernous dwelling, but she could select other fabric if she wished—as long as she made the house what Mr. Morgan called "gracious living suitable for grandchildren."

Suzy walked into a large room with a fireplace, noting the window casements were about eighteen feet high. She went up the stairs, peeking into the cold bedrooms. Lack of human warmth chilled the house, and she could understand why Josiah felt it would be better to have her family living in the house in his absence.

She decided to take the job—and first thing tomorrow, she was oiling the front door.

She was still preoccupied with those squeaky hinges when she stepped into the last room on the back hall. Like the others, it was dark and cold. Josiah had the heat in the house turned low, and for January, she would want it warmer for her babies. This back room might be suitable for her—she could make a nursery out of the room across the hall.

She screamed as something grabbed her and tossed her onto a bed. Still shrieking, she scrambled away, only to be caught in strong hands as a light flipped on.

The most handsome man she'd ever seen imprisoned her against his body. His dark eyes gleamed like a pirate's, saucily admiring his prey.

"What have we here?" he asked, pausing to allow for her answer, yet she sensed he didn't really expect or want one. Fear charged to a panicky boil inside her. "A very beautiful, very bad burglar?"

"I would never steal anything!"

He gave her a long perusal, raking her from her head to her toes and back up again. She gave him credit for not staring at her breasts, but he certainly made her feel as if he'd undressed her. She couldn't hold back a shiver.

"A trespasser, then." He slowly smiled. "I'll have to call the local police. Lucky for you I know some of the fellows here." He held her a little tighter, his wolflike gaze locked on her face.

He was toying with her. Anger-charged adrenaline made her brave; she jerked her arm free from his grasp. "I'm the new housekeeper. And since Mr. Morgan said no one would be here but me and my family, I'm pretty certain *you're* the trespasser and *I'll* be the one calling the police."

The handsome man frowned. "Well, we have a problem. I'm supposed to be living here alone, or possibly with any of my brothers, if they show up. There was never anything said about a female. I'm Josiah Morgan's third son, Dane Morgan. Who the hell are you?"

She lifted her chin. "My name is Suzy Winterstone. Your father hired me."

She could swear he backed a foot away from her.

"Suzy Winterstone?"

She nodded. "Yes." The fact that he seemed to know her name didn't appear to be a good thing.

"Pop hired you to be a housekeeper?" he demanded. *"Here?"*

She gave him a confident glare. "Yes, he did."

He stared at her for a minute and the overriding emotion she saw in those dark eyes was now anger. He frightened her; he looked like the sort of man who might not play by the rules of common decency, capable of tossing her out on the porch to soothe his temper.

"Damn Pop," he finally growled. "Just when I hoped he might be mellowing, he proves himself to be the blue ribbon–winning jackass of all time."

"Mr. Morgan has been very good to me and my family—"

He pulled her to him, kissing her hard, tasting her unrelentingly before he pushed her away. "I am *not* my father. If you choose to accept the position, be aware you'll be living here with me. And I am *not* an easy man to live with."

She forced herself not to capitulate just because his kiss had unnerved her. "I guess that's supposed to scare me. You're obviously hoping to discourage me from taking this job. I hate to dash your hopes, but Mr. Morgan wants me here, and I need the job. To be honest, I'm less afraid of you being on the premises than my babies and me being here alone." Mr. Tall, Dark and Handsome was just going to have to put up with her presence.

"Oh, yes, the babies. The pink-ribboned treasures intended to enhance my father's golden years."

"Is there a problem with that?" She looked him over, admitting to herself that he certainly was sexy, but sexy wasn't always a worthy trait in a man. "You seem to have an aversion to children, so I'm not sure why it would bother you if your father has an interest in my babies."

He shook his head, crossed his arms over his admirably broad chest. "You're forewarned that nothing that happens here between you and me will ever entail an altar or a wedding ring."

She shook her head. "You can bet your boots on that, mister. This house is big enough for the both of us, and we need never see each other. I expect wood brought in for the fireplaces—I've counted four—and I don't want muddy footprints or beer cans left about. Mr. Morgan didn't say anything about me playing house with a man or waiting on anyone hand and foot, and I will inform him of the parameters we are agreeing upon."

"*I* haven't agreed to anything."

She backed to the door before he could pounce again. Not that it had been an entirely unpleasant experience—in fact, Dane was a pretty good kisser—but her blood was still boiling like crazy at being jumped by the Adonis in the doorway. She'd never been much for hide-and-seek, so it was best to put this awkward relationship on professional footing. "You'll have to take any grievance you might have with me up with my employer."

"And no doubt Pop would side with little bitty Miss Babymaker." He stepped one foot toward her, laughed when she fled down the hall.

"Jerk," she murmured as she went down the stairs, "we'll see how hard he laughs when I short-sheet his bed and sprinkle rice in it."

If the arrogant swine thought he was going to chase her out of a well-paying job and a chance to stay home with her children, he'd find himself greatly mistaken. Some men were just too hunky for their own good—clearly Dane was suffering from too much ego.

She would set him straight.

"And we'll draw straws for bedrooms!" Suzy called up the stairs, just to assert herself more fully.

She heard his laughter echo down the hall.

Chapter Two

"So Suzy Winterstone is cute," Gabriel Morgan said to his older brother, Dane, who was visiting him and his wife, Laura, at their comfortable house. Dane had to admit, Gabriel had adapted well to living in this small domain with his growing family. But still, that just meant the youngest of all the Morgan boys had fallen under Josiah's thumb.

Dane would not be doing the same. "She's much more attractive than I would've imagined. I suppose I have to give Pop points for good taste in women." He sighed, heavily put-upon. "However, she has a bit of a mouth on her." A mouth he'd kissed, and would love to kiss again. He liked blondes, especially round, sunny ones like Suzy.

He shouldn't have done it.

Dane heard Laura laugh in the kitchen as she caught his remark. Her children—his niece and nephew—were baking sugar cookies with their mother. It was a nice way to take the edge off a cold day, and his stomach rumbled at the aroma. He sure hoped he'd be offered one of the treats.

"What kind of mouth?" Laura asked, setting a glass of milk in front of him. His hopes for being included in the cookie-tasting rose exponentially. "Pink and tempting?" she teased.

"I meant she talks a lot," he said with a mock growl, knowing his sister-in-law was giving him grief. Still, he wasn't going to admit to kissing Suzy—he'd never live it down since he'd protested his father's incessant matchmaking from the start. "She doesn't shut up."

"Hmm," Laura said, "how much could she have said in such a short amount of time? Didn't you say you only talked for about five minutes?"

"And that was plenty. During that time she set rules, gave commands and pretty much tried to show me who was going to be boss." He looked hopefully toward the kitchen, wondering if that confession had been enough to earn him a cookie.

Seeing his eager glance, Laura laughed. Gabriel chuckled.

"Penny, will you please bring your uncle Dane and your dad that platter of cookies?" Laura said. "Suzy simply sounds organized to me, Dane."

"Like someone in law enforcement, and I've had my fill of people like that." Dane took the platter from Penny gratefully. "Very pretty. How many am I allowed?" he asked Penny.

"Only two if you don't want to spoil your supper."

Penny was nearly five years old now and wise to the house rules.

"Two?" he asked, looking at Penny with his best uncle smile. "But I don't think I'm going to be getting any supper."

"That's because you didn't play your cards right with your housekeeper." Gabriel took the platter, moved two cookies to Dane's plate, three to his own, and handed the tray back to Penny. "Please put temptation out of Uncle Dane's way, honey."

She smiled at Gabriel and took the plate back to the kitchen. Her little brother, Perrin, followed, anxious for his own treat.

"How come you get three?" Dane asked. "Not that I'm trying to be ungrateful or anything, but I am older than you."

"Because I'm in good with the women of my house." Gabriel grinned. "I get extra sweets."

"Great." Dane bit the head off the sugary reindeer and closed his eyes. "She sings, Gabriel, all the time."

"Bro, she's only lived there since this morning."

"But it's nonstop. She sings to the children. The children sing back, in those little nonsense voices, and then Suzy praises them, so proud of their efforts. The noise level is pretty constant."

Laura laughed again. He considered the lightly falling snow outside, and the gray skies—both signs the temperature would be dropping. "I can't stay long.

There's wood to bring in for all four fireplaces, among other manly chores I've been assigned."

Gabriel raised his brows. "Expecting a deep freeze?"

Dane sighed. "It's just not peaceful and quiet there like I imagined it would be. Like you have here. I thought I'd be out at Pop's alone, at least until you or Pete or Jack showed up."

"I got my million dollars," Gabriel confessed. "I won't be coming, bro. You're on your own at the Morgan ranch with your trio of singing females."

Dane stared at him. "When did that happen?"

"Dad gave me my money before he went back to France."

"Because you sold out," Dane whispered, with a careful glance at Laura. "Wedding bells coaxed Pop to give in on the part about you having to live at the ranch for one year to get your money?"

Gabriel shook his head. "Nope. He just felt that I'd proven myself."

"Proven yourself?" Dane glanced around the small, clean home. "You're living in pretty tall cotton, Gabriel. Can't see that your life is all that hard."

Gabriel shook his head. "You don't get it."

Dane didn't think it was fair that Gabriel had been let off the hook. "Sucking up to Pop shouldn't be part of the deal."

"Why?" Gabriel looked at him. "All Dad wants is family harmony."

"And grandchildren!" Dane tried to sound horrified

and maybe even accusative—Gabriel had definitely sold out, the weasel—but looking at Laura's gently rounded stomach made it a bit hard to be completely indignant.

The fact was, Gabriel had done what Dane, Pete and Jack didn't want to do. Jack would never make up with Pop, not after Pop kicked him out for luring his too-young brothers to the rodeo all those years ago. Dane and Pete still harbored enough bad feelings to fill a valley. Still, he couldn't fault Gabriel. "Never mind," Dane said, morosely finishing off his cookies. "The baby always has it the easiest."

He brushed off the crumbs and stood to leave. Laura handed him a lace napkin full of cookies to take with him. He headed to the door, glanced around at Gabriel and his family and the life he'd chosen. Then he tipped his hat to Laura, kissed both the children, thanked them for sharing their delicious cookies, and braced himself for the cold outside.

It was nothing, he knew, like the cold he was going to get at the ranch. He only had three hundred sixty-four more days to go. It wasn't a lifetime, something he'd already felt he'd lived.

He'd retired from the Texas Rangers following years of service. After enlisting in the military—just to get away from Pop—Dane had gotten his college degree, then moved on. He went into the police academy, becoming a top recruit. With his competitive nature, he'd pushed himself hard enough to make it into the Rangers.

And then, at twenty-eight, he'd burned out. He'd seen the worst in people while on the job, but always felt he had his friends to fall back on, no matter what. The final straw was his best friend talking him out of his life savings. Dane realized he wasn't as much of a tough guy as he thought he was, and began to doubt his ability to see the good in people.

Suzy seemed good, but she sure had dug her way into an old man's life with ease. Pop was supposed to be a tough guy, too.

Maybe Morgans were just easy marks for a sad story. He'd find out in the next year of hell with the rule-making Miss Winterstone.

He got into his truck, carefully placing the cookies on the seat next to his so they wouldn't break. On the other hand, there was something to be said for sucking up, he decided. Yet, he wasn't sure he could survive three hundred sixty-four more days in a house with a woman he'd kissed, since he frequently found himself wondering about kissing her again.

He'd always been a bit of a rebel, something that irked Pop no end. The practically neon sign the little mother was wearing that said No Trespassing made him definitely want to jump the fence.

But knowing Pop would be rewarded for his manipulative ways, Dane vowed to give up trespassing, at least where Suzy was concerned. He'd refused to even look at the babies this morning—he knew that if he wasn't careful, he could get sucked into a life just like Gabriel's.

It was all about the children, and Dane understood the game.

SUZY PUT HER TWO TODDLERS down for a nap, then lay beside them, rubbing their backs as they snuggled into the bed comforter. She'd chosen the large back bedroom for herself and the children. It was big enough for them to sleep in the same room with her. That way, if she needed to get up in the night to check on them, she wouldn't risk running into Mr. Loves-the-Dark Ranger. She didn't trust him, not one bit. He'd probably jump out and grab her again just for the pleasure of hearing her yelp. And he'd made it obvious this morning that he didn't want her there—he hadn't spoken a word to her. Not even a polite good morning. So she'd sung to keep the frosty awkwardness in check.

"Fine by me," she told the girls. "It's better when he's not around being pigheaded."

The babies slept on without heeding her comment. She'd named the eighteen-month-old girls Nicole and Sandra after her mother. For the hundredth time, she thought about calling her mother, then decided it wouldn't be a good idea. Her mother, who lived in Fort Wylie, had told Suzy in no uncertain terms that being pregnant and unmarried was a disgrace. Her mother and father were scions of Fort Wylie and reputation mattered to them. Appearances were important.

Suzy's appearance was one of loose living, her mother had said, and they hadn't spoken since. She'd never visited the hospital to see the newborns. It killed Suzy, broke her heart, but it was her mother's right to feel as she did. "I wasn't delighted when your father packed up, either," she murmured to her daughters. "I didn't foresee Frank being so afraid of responsibility."

He'd liked her well enough for her family's money—but when he'd realized that the Winterstones were, well, wintry about their new grandchildren, cutting off even Suzy's trust fund she would have received at age thirty, well, Frank had disappeared like a puff of dust under a vacuum cleaner.

"Speaking of vacuums," she said, closing her eyes, "just as soon as we finish our beauty rest, girls, we need to lug that monstrous canister up here and vacuum all the rooms thoroughly. Don't think it's been done in thirty years."

She hadn't planned on napping, but the wind was howling outside, the snow sugaring the ground, and at the moment, she felt so blessed lying on the bed with her children that she drifted off to sleep.

DANE WALKED IN WITH A LOAD of firewood, and remembering Suzy's caution about dirtying up the floors, swept off the snow and ice as best he could from the logs and his boots. Last thing he wanted was a further discourse on his cleanliness. He carried the wood upstairs. There were two fireplaces up, plus two downstairs. He'd take care of the upper level fireplaces first, particularly in his room. It was a great night for a nice, cozy fire in the hearth in Pop's bedroom, which he had decided to commandeer for himself as the only son in residence.

He deserved some of the finer things in life. One, for

living in this godforsaken backwater and, two, for having Suzy and her tiny crew cast upon him.

At the door of the bedroom, he stopped in his tracks. On his bed lay Suzy, her two little angels sleeping soundly beside her. Well, they weren't angels, they were more like time bombs, he reminded himself, backing into the hallway. Set to explode his world, drawing him in with their cherubic faces. Tingles ran over his arms. He allowed himself to give Suzy a thorough, yet lightning-fast once-over, avoiding the pink-wrapped dolls beside her.

"Holy smokes, that was close." He went down the hall, placed the firewood in the stacker in the smaller bedroom. What the hell was she doing in his room? On his bed? She couldn't stay there, that was for certain. Somehow he was going to have to explain to her that she just couldn't fall asleep on the job, cushy employment though it was, in the first available reclining apparatus she came upon. His bed should be his domain—and anyway, hadn't she already read him the riot act about how she was never stepping in his room?

His heart thundered in his chest. Pop stayed in France almost year-round, giving the boys a lot of time to gnash their teeth over his wily proposal. Dane was proud that he'd been wilier. Pop believed that money would buy love, like castles in France and sandboxes in the Caribbean, but Dane knew money and love were not always good bed partners.

Dane intended to tell Goldilocks when she awakened

that his bed was not "just right" for her. She could just stick that in her proverbial little pipe and move into a smaller, less-appointed chamber.

No. Sighing, he knew he wouldn't do that. There were three of her family and only one of him. Besides, he could be a gentleman if it was absolutely required, and in Suzy's case, it probably was. Besides, he didn't actually need the gold-outfitted bidet and tub Pop had in his master bath; he didn't need the slipper sofa by the hearth, nor the lush rugs underfoot surrounding the massive canopied bed. One of the other starker, less decked-out rooms would be fine for him—like this one.

Restlessly he rose to light a fire in the small fireplace. The tinder caught slowly, the cold, damp logs reluctant to take the heat.

He realized that no matter how much he fought it, staying on the ranch for a year was not going to be the easiest assignment he'd ever had. He'd talked himself into this "cream puff" of a situation, but Pop would certainly laugh if he saw him now, cowed into a small bedroom and padding around with clean, silent feet, all thanks to Pop and his Grandchildren Conspiracy.

Chapter Three

In the morning, Suzy was awakened by her children stirring. Nicole gently touched her mother's face. Sandra waved a tiny hand at some sunlight streaming into the room. Suzy smiled, enjoying the gentle wake up. "You must be getting hungry," she told her girls, and then realized they had slept the entire night in the house without any incident concerning Dane Morgan. "This is going to work just fine," she said, putting on her clothes.

She helped her daughters dress, a slow process because they were at the age when they wanted to do things themselves. Their little fingers weren't quite ready for pulling on tights to keep their legs warm, or brushing their own hair. Finally, they were all ready to leave the sanctuary of their bedroom and head into the kitchen.

"Hold my hands," she told her girls. "We have to be very careful on these stairs." She tiptoed by the other bedrooms on the hall in order to avoid a run-in with Josiah's son, breathing much easier when she made it to the kitchen.

But the dark-haired, cold-eyed handsome stranger sitting at the table pulled a startled shriek from her. He jumped to his feet, spilling hot coffee on his hand and swearing a blue streak. Her daughters began to cry so she clutched them to her, glaring at the stranger. "Who are you?"

"Who are you?" he demanded. "You don't live here."

She raised her chin. "I do live here. And if you don't leave right this instant, I'll scream. There's a man sleeping upstairs and he'll come running down—"

The back door opened. "It's durn cold out—" Dane stopped when he saw the scene in the kitchen. His gaze swept over her, registering her panic, and then went to the stranger. He calmly walked over to the sink to wash his hands.

Suzy gasped. "What are you doing?"

"Washing my hands to warm them up." Dane smiled at her. "Is there a problem?"

She blinked. "Do you know this person?"

The man took off his hat, nodding to her. "My name's Pete. I'm one of Dane's brothers," he explained. "I let myself in," he said to Dane who merely nodded. "I apologize if I frightened you." He gave Suzy what she supposed was a reassuring smile. "Dane says I unnerve him when I pop in, too. I didn't realize he had company."

"I am not his company," Suzy said, stiffening. "I'm the housekeeper."

Pete grinned hugely. "Pop," he said to Dane. "He's got you by the short—"

"Ah, let's get some breakfast on the table," Dane interrupted. "Is that in your job description?" he asked Suzy. "I'm not quite sure of all the parameters yet."

These two were quite the pair. There was some unspoken joke going on between them, but Suzy was in no mood to guess what it was. "I cook for myself and my daughters," she said, getting out a box of oatmeal. "You two are on your own."

She waited for Dane to move away from the sink so she could fill a pot with water. He looked at the pot a trifle regretfully before turning to his brother.

"We're still working out the kinks in this housekeeping thing," he said, and Pete nodded.

"I see that." Pete slouched into his chair and put his feet up on another one, making himself right at home. Suzy's irritation rose, because, after all, it was his home and she hadn't factored being in a house with one man much less two. But no one had been on the ranch in six months—surely both of these men weren't planning on staying long.

"Hope I won't be any trouble," Pete said.

Suzy whirled to look at him, ignoring how fast her heart had begun to beat as she'd stood next to Dane at the sink. "Trouble?"

"Living here."

Dane grinned. "Come to sweat it out for your share?"

Pete shrugged. His gaze went to Suzy for just an instant. "Hadn't planned on it, but you two need a chaperone. Pop clearly didn't consider that in his scheming, but I might be persuaded."

Suzy's daughters stared up at the big man, completely perplexed by the presence of two males. They hadn't been around many, and the Morgan men had deep voices and large, masculine presences. Suzy decided to skip the chaperone comment and went straight to the ominous word in Pete's analysis. *"Scheming?"*

"You know. To get you two to fall in love with each other."

Suzy froze. "Are you implying that my job is nothing more than a sham? A cover to induce me into playing house with your brother so that we'd somehow end up together?"

Dane winced. "That might be putting it a bit bluntly—"

"Actually, I think she nailed Pop's plan," Pete said. "That seems to be the gist of it."

"Now that we're all feeling very awkward, why don't we eat some oatmeal? Matters will probably seem less complicated on full stomachs." Dane glanced longingly at the pot Suzy still held in her hand.

Suzy frowned. "Let me be perfectly clear on something. I am not here for anyone's amusement. Nor did your father seem like the type to be so underhanded. I'm shocked you would suggest it," she said to Pete. "And I'm annoyed that you don't refute it," she told Dane.

Both brothers shrugged.

"I think you two are troublemakers," Suzy said, "and if you're trying to run me out of this house to spite your father, a man I know neither of you got along with, I

suggest you take your problems up with Mr. Morgan."
She took a deep breath, set the pot on the stove. "Now
if you'll excuse me, I'm going to feed my children."

Suzy felt her hands tremble ever so slightly. Nicole
and Sandra clung to her legs, probably sensing the
tension in the room. She had a good mind to call Mr.
Morgan and directly ask him what his sons were up to—
but decided against it just as quickly. A check had been
included with the letter in which Mr. Morgan had hired
her, with a very generous three months' salary.

She'd deposited the check. For the first time, she
was feeling more comfortable financially. Mr. Morgan
had given each of her children what he called inheri-
tances, money that was tucked away in savings accounts
for their education. What business arrangements existed
between Mr. Morgan and herself were none of his sons'
business. It was the brothers' fault if they felt uncomfortable around her—they should be ashamed of the
stories they'd concocted about their own father!

"Suzy, maybe we jumped to conclusions," Dane said.
She ignored that and went on stirring oatmeal into the
pot. "You don't know Pop like we do, though."

"It doesn't matter. Your story is implausible. There's
no way your father knew you'd be here, Dane. You
didn't even know Pete was coming to stay." She glanced
at him. "I don't want to be dragged into your family
issues, and from the way I see it, you have issues with
your father. He doesn't really have them with you."

Dane and Pete stared at her, their jaws slightly slack.

She could tell she had shocked them—but wasn't that a good thing? These men were taking some childish anger out on an old man who cared for them deeply. "It's none of my concern," she said, putting brown sugar and butter into bowls. "Let's just go on like none of this ever happened." Even though it had already been said—and Dane had even kissed her! "As far as Pete's idea of a chaperone, it's a good one. I'll take care of that."

Dane didn't look too happy, and Pete seemed to realize he'd caused his brother some type of predicament, but what he didn't realize was that Suzy herself had been reminded of her own mother's direct criticism of her "looseness." Suzy was an embarrassment to her wealthy family. She glanced at the brothers—too handsome and too cocky for their own good!—as she seated her daughters at the table and put their bowls in front of them.

Without another glance at the men staring hungrily at the children's breakfast, Suzy began humming under her breath.

PETE SIGHED AS HE AND HIS brother went out to one of the barns. "Sorry if I'm cramping your love nest. I assumed you'd be alone."

Dane held in a groan. "I didn't realize I had company, either, until yesterday. Needless to say, Pop's probably laughing in the French countryside, enjoying the grapes and the excellent cuisine."

"I bet. You know, I've never liked this place. It was

never a home. We were too far from town to have friends, and Pop was too busy to be a father. I wouldn't even be here if it wasn't for the money."

"Got yourself in a bind?" Dane asked curiously, and Pete nodded.

"You, too?"

"Yeah," Dane said, thinking about his partner. "You'd think with Pop as a role model, I wouldn't have gotten sucked into a con game, but I did. Lost my savings." Dane shook his head. "And now it seems we're getting sucked into another."

"Not me," Pete said. "I never got a letter from Pop asking me to look out for a woman. I figure I'm in the clear by now."

Dane shook his head. "If I were you, I'd be even more wary."

Pete stopped in the motion of slinging a saddle across a wooden horse. "What's that supposed to mean?"

"I've always feared the unknown most with Pop." Dane grinned at his brother, enjoying the chance to have the upper hand, if only for a moment. "I know what my full downside is—Suzy. The other shoe has yet to drop for you."

"Maybe Suzy's *my* dream girl," Pete said, then laughed at Dane's shocked expression. "Oh, come on, Pop's not picky about who pairs up with whom, just as long as we pair up with some woman and provide him with grandchildren."

Dane stopped his work to give his brother a full glaring. "What is a secret agent going to do with a wife?"

"Be very happy," Pete said. "I'm thinking about settling down."

Dane laughed. "Like hell you are." His brother was only thirty and still had the call of the wild written all over him. Tough and sinewy, with glacial dark eyes and cheeks sculpted by demons—at least that's what Pop had always said—Pete was no ladies' man.

No man for a lady, and certainly not for a lady like Suzy.

"Feel like a gentle wager?" Pete asked.

Dane raised a brow. "As a former Texas Ranger, I should say no, but curiosity compels me to ask what you have in mind."

"Suzy falls for me, and you owe me a night of baby-sitting her little angels so I can romance their mother."

"That's heinous," Dane said, feeling a flicker of jealousy that shook him. "Betting on a woman's feelings is ungentlemanly."

Pete laughed. "Bro, you're taking a leaf out of Gabriel's book."

"Meaning?"

"You're already down for the count."

Dane snorted and grabbed some neatsfoot oil to clean and shine the saddle. He completely ignored Pete and his dumb observation. The thing that Pete didn't know was Dane was moving to Mexico where the palm trees waved and the sun shone hot, the tortillas were soft and the ladies were sweet. He hated Texas and nothing—and no one—was ever going to entice him to stay for long.

Unlike Pete, whose job chasing international baddies might be wearing thin. Maybe Pete's wandering feet *were* beginning to cool off.

"Listen, Pete," he said suddenly and abruptly, as if to underline his own mental game, "If you're frustrated and lonely and looking for a good time, by all means, put on your best show for Suzy. And I might add she's probably not the only single woman in town. Best part is, these days all roads lead to town pretty quickly, and you've got a shiny truck to get you there for all the womanizing you can stand during your break."

Pete laughed and went looking for something in the barn. Dane put the whole incident out of his mind for a moment, then took a pocketknife out of his back pocket. With a careful stroke, he notched two lines on the wood rail beside the saddle.

Only three hundred sixty-three more days to go.

CRICKET JASPER HAD KNOWN Suzy Winterstone a long time, and if Suzy said she needed help, then Suzy needed help. So without hesitation Cricket packed her bags and headed out from Fort Wylie to spend a week with Suzy at an old house in the deep country.

Cricket wasn't sure why Suzy wouldn't come back to Fort Wylie. The Winterstones weren't the most affectionate clan, but that they missed their only daughter, Cricket was certain. They were still mad about the unplanned pregnancy, but that was over two years past. Surely it was time to put all those hot emotions in the past.

Cricket could feel forgiveness since she was a deacon. And Suzy was like a sister to her—she wanted Suzy to be happy. Family matters weren't important at the moment, Cricket decided, and parked her little Volkswagen beside the two big trucks in the Morgan ranch driveway, and the smaller, older car that Cricket recognized as Suzy's.

Suzy came out on the porch, waiting with a big smile and her two little girls beside her. Cricket hadn't seen the girls since they were born—just tiny babies—so she hurried to sweep them into her arms. "I'm so glad to see you, Suzy. And these two little dumplings!"

Suzy smiled, grateful her friend had arrived. "Thank you so much for coming out."

"No problem," Cricket told her with a hug. "The minute you said you needed help, I penciled in vacation time…." Her words trailed off as two large men walked toward the house from an outlying barn. "My goodness, they grow them big in the country, don't they?"

Suzy frowned. "At least the Morgans seem to be larger than life. They're the reason I need help."

"They live here?" Cricket's eyes were huge.

She nodded. "You'll quickly understand why their father despairs of them."

"Well, I—" Cricket glanced at the men again. "Do you have to live here with them?"

"I didn't know they'd be here when I took the position. I've deposited my three months' salary, and frankly, I need the money. Not to mention I was eager to find a position where I could stay home with my children while they're so young."

"Three months," Cricket murmured.

"Oh, they'll be here a year," Suzy told her. "Dane was here first, then Pete showed up, suggesting I needed a chaperone."

Cricket gasped. "The nerve!"

"I think it's a good idea." Suzy eyed the men as they approached the porch. "Something also tells me I need an objective opinion of my situation."

"And you think my eyes are objective?" Cricket gave the men a thorough once-over. "Looks like you're living in heaven on earth to me."

"Hello," Pete said to Cricket, a grin lighting his face, although Suzy had to admit that Dane's expression was just as impressed. Tall and dark to Suzy's more cheerful blond roundness, Cricket caught and held every man's eye. She had a long, lean graceful body, a sweet smile and big brown eyes—a tall Audrey Hepburn with her own independent carriage.

Men found the combination alluring. But Cricket had never been interested in much outside her church duties.

"This is Cricket Jasper, my best friend and Nicole's and Sandra's godmother," Suzy said, smiling at the men's dumbstruck expressions. "She's going to stay with me for a week. Stay with us," she amended, not feeling the slightest bit guilty for putting such luscious bait in front of the two very large tomcats.

"Your chaperone, I presume?" Pete said, grinning at Suzy. "Nice. I mean, it's nice to meet you, Cricket."

But Dane shot Suzy a glare. "While it's nice to meet you, Cricket, and you're welcome at the Morgan ranch, please round out our happy foursome in a guest capacity. I personally do not require a chaperone—*for any reason.*"

Chapter Four

"Whew," Pete said as Dane stomped into the house, "please pardon my brother's boneheaded manners. Texas doesn't agree with him, and some days he's a wee bit moody." Then he whispered to Cricket, "It passes by noon. On his better days."

Suzy looked at Pete. "Did I mention Cricket is a deacon in her church?"

Pete blinked. "So she *is* a chaperone."

"Yes," Suzy said, dragging her friend away. "Come on, before you fall under the spell."

Cricket followed willingly. "I don't think it was a spell. I'm immune to those. I think it was shock. Not sure I've ever seen so much man in one pair of boots."

"It's okay," Suzy said. "The feeling will pass once you realize that they're bona fide womanizers."

"Too bad," Cricket said. "You know who'd be perfect for that lanky one back on the porch?"

Suzy stopped, gathering her girls to her. "I'm afraid to ask."

"Priscilla Perkins."

Suzy glanced up at Cricket. "The Priscilla Perkins whom you despised on sight because she lured your brother away from his fiancée?"

"That was Thad's fault," Cricket said. "He should have had stronger morals. But men and morals are not always secure friends, and heaven knows Priscilla has more than her share of charms."

Suzy shook her head. "I wouldn't wish either of these men even on Priscilla Perkins." Actually, Dane was the kind of man she'd hate to see Priscilla throw her cap at, because he was darling in a sort of hotheaded, sexy way. And he'd kissed her, which she hated to admit had been the hottest kiss she'd ever experienced. But truthfully, Dane was all knotted up and probably had no idea how he'd got that way. Pete seemed like he was meant for wild times and outrageous women—an explosive combination at best.

"Are there any more of them?" Cricket helped Suzy take the girls out back where a patch of sunlight was barely warming the January-cold grass. "The brothers?"

"The youngest, Gabriel, is married and lives close to town. Mr. Morgan was thrilled about the wedding—he's crazy about Laura and her children. I've never met Gabriel, but he's not as mulish as his brothers, apparently." Suzy smiled. "And Mr. Morgan mentioned an eldest son whom he never sees, with whom he has a difficult relationship." She looked at Cricket, sympathy in her eyes as she picked out a ball for the girls to try to roll. "I could tell it hurt him a lot that he and Jack are estranged."

"How did you meet Mr. Morgan?"

"I was a nurse at the hospital when Mr. Morgan was brought in one day. He has—" she lowered her voice and glanced around to make certain there were no Morgan men around "—some health issues."

Cricket's eyes went wide. "His sons don't know?"

Suzy shook her head. "He doesn't want them to know. He's hoping they'll all come home and want to stay one day."

"Be a family."

"At least try." Suzy looked at her little girls with pleasure. "I can't argue with the plan. My mother and father certainly have no desire whatsoever to be a family."

Cricket winced. "I think they regret some of their words—"

"Don't." Suzy rose, taking the ball with her. It was now the middle of the afternoon. She needed to put the girls down for a quick nap and start their dinner. "Unlike Mr. Morgan, I don't believe in fairy tales."

Cricket's eyes went wide. "Suzy!"

"Why don't you bring in your luggage," Suzy said, unwilling to think about the past. "I plan to enjoy every moment of your time here, so first I'm going to show you to a room, and then put the girls down to nap, and then you and I are going to sit and girl chat."

A window opened on the second floor. Dane poked his head out, staring down at them. Suzy was pretty sure the lord of the manor's mood hadn't improved any by the scowl on his face.

"Can I assume you've commandeered the master suite?"

Suzy put her hands on her hips. "You may assume that."

"And where is Cricket sleeping?"

"In the room next to mine."

"I can sleep wherever," Cricket said hurriedly. "Suzy, I don't want to put anyone out."

"This place is like a castle. There are plenty of rooms. Let me see what his problem really is." She returned his scowl. "Why do you care where Cricket sleeps?"

"I don't. Pete wants to know."

Suzy looked at Cricket. "It's all about communication."

"He just wants to know where he should sleep," Dane explained. "He didn't know you were in Pop's old room."

"I took the master because it was big enough for me and the girls, and your father said I should since he wasn't planning on returning any time soon. And besides, there's a huge lock on the door. He said I'd be safer that way."

Dane considered that. "Are you saying you've spoken to my father recently?"

She nodded. "Yesterday afternoon after you left. I wanted him to know I was accepting the job."

"You didn't tell him I was here, did you?"

"I mentioned it," Suzy said, not sure why it mattered. "Is there a problem?"

"There are problems," Dane said, "but they're really not your concern." He slammed the window down.

Cricket looked at her. "Those boys are a symphony in human frailty."

Suzy laughed. "I'm so glad you're here. Let's go get you settled."

The window shot back up. "Now, listen," Dane said, "did my father tell you about the nice strong lock on the bedroom door before or after you told him I was here?"

She shrugged. "Before. He said he'd feel better knowing the girls and I were tightly locked up since we're so far out in the country. Why?"

He thought about that, seeming satisfied after a moment. "Just checking." The window shut again. Suzy looked at Cricket, who shrugged.

"Think you'll last a year?" Cricket asked. "I'm not sure I could swim in all these undercurrents."

"I'll last," Suzy said. "Swimming's my only choice."

"WHAT EXACTLY DOES A DEACON DO?" Dane asked Pete as they did chores in the barn.

"Depends," Pete said, "marry you, bury you, discuss spiritual stuff with you and so forth. Why? Got a thing for Deacon Cricket?"

"No!" Dane slid a glance at his brother. "Do you?"

Pete sighed. "I would, if I was able. But since I'm not, I don't torture myself. I'm looking for a peachy blonde."

Since Suzy probably qualified as a "peachy blonde,"

Dane didn't want more information than that. "So, are you really hanging around here for a while?"

"Sure. What's better than family?" Pete grinned. "As long as Pop's not around, that is."

"Jack planning on showing up?"

"Wouldn't bet the farm on that ever happening."

Dane moved some tack to the other end of the barn while he digested his thoughts. "Since you're the only one who really knows how to find Jack, why don't you tell him the old man isn't here and he might as well pay a call on the rest of us slobs? We'll get Gabriel and Laura out here, let everybody have a grand old time getting to know each other again. Not that I'm suggesting we go overboard to please Pop but, hell, I'm ready to see the king of the rodeo."

"Nah," Pete said, "don't think it would work."

"Why? Tell Jack to start the New Year off right with a little family, a little—"

"Dane, dude. It's not going to happen." Pete shook his head.

"I guess there's a reason," Dane said, and his brother nodded.

"Yeah. Jack's sworn to never set foot on the Morgan ranch again."

Dane whistled. "No million dollars for him."

"Jack wouldn't give a da—"

"Hey, fellows!" Suzy poked her head into the barn. Both men straightened, surprised. "Cricket and I and the girls are going to walk around town."

"Sounds like a party," Dane said, realizing he sounded

smart-alecky but not meaning it that way. Why did everything he said around Suzy seem to come out stupid?

"It is a party. Toddlers, a deacon and a single mom. Wild girls."

"Yeah, well," Dane said, "Pete and I were never much for wild women."

Everyone in the barn stood still, the fib seeming to take a shape of its own. "I suppose you have underwater land you'd like to sell me, too," Suzy said, "but what I was really wondering was if you want to accompany us."

"Sure," Pete said, dropping what he'd been doing, which was pretty much nothing, in Dane's opinion. He glanced at Dane. "Nothing pressing around here, right, brother?"

He wanted to go, but at what price to his conscience? Dane knew what his father was up to. Wasn't it best if he and Suzy stayed well away from each other? She was an innocent party—she really seemed to have no idea what Pop had intended. She claimed Pop was totally innocent.

Dane knew better. "I don't know," he said. "I'm not a going-out kind of guy."

Pete thumped him on the back. "That's cool. You stay in, and I'll make sure the girls and dolls stay warm and cozy and safe. I haven't seen Union Junction in a long time," he told Suzy as he walked out of the barn with her. "I'm sure there's tons of changes I need to catch up on while we give Cricket the grand tour."

Alone in the barn, Dane grimaced. Pete was unusually friendly, and he couldn't tell what was up with that. Was his brother flirting with the single mother or the deacon—and did he care? "I *don't* care," he muttered.

"Dane?" Suzy said, glancing in the barn again. "We're going to get hot chocolate in town. Sure you don't want to come along?"

What the hell. He did, and he was tired of acting like he didn't. Hot chocolate was harmless, right? "As long as Pete's paying," he said, and went to join the party.

TWO HOURS LATER, DANE was pretty sure hot chocolate was going to be his undoing. Pete flirted outrageously with both women—he apparently saw no reason to acknowledge his brother—and Suzy and Cricket seemed to eat up the attention. Nor could Dane make any strides with the toddlers, Nicole and Sandra, because there was Pete, making suck-up points by helping them cool their hot cocoa, or carrying the girls on his shoulders so that they could better see into shop windows as the group walked down the main street of Union Junction.

Dane didn't even know why he was out of sorts. Something suspiciously like jealousy ate at his insides, which felt uncomfortably like worms crawling around inside him, fat and cold and slithery.

He wanted to be mad at Pete, but he knew he was really mad at himself. Having gotten off on the wrong foot with Suzy in the very beginning, he didn't appreciate further distance being made between them, and particularly by his older brother.

Competition had never been his downfall before. But he had to admit that his relationships with men were lacking in the trust area. He didn't trust Pop, and he'd made the mistake of trusting his former partner, Kenny, and lost his shirt for that. Worst of all, Jack was nowhere to be seen. Maybe he needed a good example of how a man should act around a woman with two children, but to Dane's mind, the chivalrous thing to do was to keep distance between them. They had no future because he was retiring young to Mexico where it was warm all year round, not like Union Junction. He was certain a bad example to follow was Pete's, acting as if he was some kind of woman magnet, irresistible to the opposite sex.

What really dug at him was how much all four girls seemed to enjoy the attention. *I'm sulking,* he realized. *An old habit of being the third son. No wonder I hate Texas. I really hate being third in a family of dysfunctional freaks.*

Okay, that was harsh. The Morgans weren't freaks; they just had more than their share of cautionary tales. So what? A man bucked up and took it.

He could take it. Couldn't he?

And besides, it was all none of his business. Pete could do what he liked, and so could Suzy. He sighed to himself, deciding he was as much fun as a holey sock. Pete, with his older, hard-won maturity, would seem more impressive to a woman who craved some sort of adventure in her life.

Of course, if Suzy wanted adventure, then he was Mr. Adventure in the amazing flesh. "Before I went into law enforcement," he said, "I thought I'd probably have to stay in the military forever to stay out of trouble."

Suzy and Cricket paused in their walking to look at him. Pete frowned, not liking the limelight being off him all of a sudden.

"We were an indulgent group of boys," Dane said. "I wanted to be just like Jack when I grew up. I couldn't, so I did crazy stuff like canoeing through Mexico and parachuting out in California until I realized I had to grow up. The military changed me, and then being a Ranger gave me purpose in life."

Suzy smiled at him. "No wonder you seem so ready to settle down."

Dane felt his bravado slip. "Settle down?"

Cricket nodded. "Suzy and I have decided we've never seen a man so ready to marry and start a family."

Pete was grinning like mad. Dane perked up under the women's admiring eyes, though his courage wanted to take a major hike. "I plan on settling down in Mexico next year, as a matter of fact."

"Oh. Mexico?" Suzy said, sounding surprised, and maybe unpleasantly so.

"Cost of living's great," he explained. "I figure if Pop can live in France and all over the world, I should at least be able to park my boots in a border country."

"I guess so," Suzy said.

Cricket nodded. "It makes sense."

They turned their attention back to Pete, who was grinning at him like a stupid hyena. The three of them, along with the tiny toddlers, one of which was held by Pete and one by Cricket, continued walking along the sidewalk. There wasn't enough room for him, unless he wanted to walk in the street, which he didn't, because that would feel as if he wasn't part of the group—a mere hanger-on pedestrian. Didn't Pete have some secret agent-spy stuff he needed to attend to? Dane wondered sourly.

Some chaperone Cricket was turning out to be—more like the fairy matchmaker. Suzy was supposed to be his responsibility, according to Pop's instructions—those very same instructions he'd cursorily read last June and then shuffled onto an intermediate, he recalled. And then he'd headed off for six months, keeping himself well away from the mother and her twins. Thwarting Pop was great, but he didn't like Pete weaseling in on his assignment.

He let himself think up the most impressive thing he could possibly hope to say to a group like this.

"Let's go to the rodeo tomorrow," he suggested, and with Pete gesturing No to him, it was like a comet he could latch on to with joy. "Anybody up for watching cowboys get thrown in Lonely Hearts Station?"

"That sounds like so much fun!" Suzy exclaimed. Cricket nodded enthusiastically, but Pete's lips turned down in a tight frown.

Dane clapped him on the back. "Remember when you wanted to grow up to be a rodeo clown?"

"At least one of us has achieved clown status," Pete said.

"We'd best get back," Suzy said, "the girls are

starting to get a little fussy. And we want to be well rested for the rodeo tomorrow."

"What's the problem?" Dane asked Pete under his breath. "It's just harmless fun." Of course, that's what he'd thought about tonight's outing, and look where it had gotten him: showboating into another outing with Suzy.

Not with Suzy—with the group, he told the mocking voice chiding him.

"If you're smart," Pete said as the ladies walked ahead of them, "you'll figure out what you're going to do to cure the case of hots scorching your brain."

"What do you mean?" Dane demanded, but Pete just shook his head.

"Knucklehead," Dane said as Pete galloped off with Sandra on his shoulders, "you just want every woman for yourself."

He understood himself well enough to know that the family closeness and brotherly harmony his father dreamed of wasn't going to happen if he and Pete hit a rough patch because of a woman.

The best thing he could do was to forget about Suzy and her twins altogether.

"At least I still have Mexico," he muttered, and then wondered why the idea of palm trees in January didn't seem quite as exciting as it once had.

Chapter Five

That evening, after tucking the little girls in bed, Suzy and Cricket sat sharing a pot of hot tea in the Morgan ranch kitchen. Suzy stirred sugar into her cup. "Any regrets for coming out here?"

Cricket grinned. "It's been a productive day. You could have warned me what handsome rascals the Morgan brothers are."

Suzy shook her head. "I had a handsome rascal. He turned out to be a weasel."

Cricket nodded. "Pete and Dane don't seem all that steadfast, either. But they have some good points."

"Fortunately, I'm not in the market, so it doesn't matter." Suzy glanced around, glad that the men had gone out to the barn. Heaven only knew what they were doing there, in the darkness of one of the coldest January nights on record. "Neither of them strikes me as father material, anyway."

"You never talk to your old fiancé?"

"No. It's not like I shut the door on Frank to deliberately keep him away from Nicole and Sandra. But he made it clear he wasn't interested in being a father." Suzy was sad for her children, but his desertion was really no different from her parents' feelings. She'd chosen to go into parenthood alone. It wasn't a decision she regretted for even a fraction of a second. "The girls have a wonderful godmother in you, though," Suzy said, smiling so that Cricket wouldn't know how sad she felt about her girls' father and grandparents.

"It must be hard for you, Suzy," Cricket murmured.

"My life is so much better since the girls were born. They make me laugh, they make me smile, they give me focus. There's nothing I want more than to see them grow up to be happy and loved."

"I want children," Cricket admitted, "but not necessarily a husband. Does that sound awful?"

"Not to me," Suzy said, "but the church might be concerned."

Cricket smiled. "What I meant was, I believe I could handle the responsibilities that go along with children better than I could handle a man. Your girls are such angels."

Suzy felt surrounded by a warm glow over the mention of her babies. "Don't let the Morgan men hear you say you want children." Suzy thought about how far away from her girls Dane managed to stay. Pete, on the other hand, seemed more than happy to play stand-in uncle. "Supposedly there's a Grandchildren Conspiracy, to hear Dane tell it."

"Oh. No worries on that score." Cricket smiled. "Your kids are enough for me for now. But what about you? What do you dream of?"

Suzy hesitated. Her family was cold, aloof from each other. She'd spent hours watching family TV shows where the characters were happy being close-knit, supportive and affectionate. "I'd love more children."

Cricket lifted her teacup in a cheers motion. "My hat is off to you."

Suzy shook her head. "Put your hat back on. I said I'd love them, not that I plan to have more."

"Suzy, why don't you take the girls by to see your parents?" Cricket asked, her voice soft.

Suzy shook her head. "My folks are the complete opposite of Mr. Morgan. Children born out of wedlock are not welcome."

Cricket hesitated, then sighed. "Don't you think that if your parents just saw the girls, saw how adorable and sweet they are—"

"The girls and I are a family, and that's enough." Suzy didn't mean to be rude by cutting off Cricket's encouragement, but her friend couldn't possibly understand how impossible some bridges were to cross.

JOSIAH MORGAN KNEW SOMETHING about being alone. It was why he wanted his boys to have loving marriages and children to comfort them in their old age. When his wife left him and the boys behind all those years ago, he'd tasted the bitter, galling taste of rejection. When his boys left him, he'd been shattered by the knowledge that he was an utter failure.

Was that too simple? Hell, no. Josiah knew it deep in his bones. He'd lost a good wife, he'd made his own children hate him. There was nothing painless about that.

It took a very hard-hearted man to realize he was an unlikable human being.

When his wife left, he'd accepted it without complaint. A woman was a free-willed creature. In spite of his best efforts to make Giselle happy, it had taken him many years to realize his best efforts were not pointed in the right direction. His passion had been to make himself happy as he built worlds outside of his home. She had responded by returning to France.

He'd had no choice but to accept it.

But his boys' desertion—that had forced a mirror of self-reflection on him that he could not escape, an image that was harsh and destined to be lonely.

Still, he knew no other way to be. The boys had done wrong, scaring him by sneaking out to watch Jack at the rodeo. They could have been killed in that car accident.

They couldn't understand the deep fear fathers suffered—particularly single fathers. They would never know the bone-deep terror a man could feel at the prospect of losing his children when he had nothing else in life he loved.

It was true. Josiah Morgan was a man who saw his

real riches in terms of his four boys, but it had taken them leaving for him to realize it.

Now it was too late. Life's clock ticked by inexorably, stealing the bits of time he had left to be a father. He'd probably burn in hell for being such an earthly failure. Certainly he'd not be awarded angel's wings.

So he'd added to his sins by meddling. Could meddling be considered a sin? He thought it would be by his sons. Yet Gabriel seemed happy in the end with his father's matchmaking. Would they ever understand he only wanted them to have the one thing money couldn't buy—love?

Now he had to work on Dane and Pete. They'd be harder than Gabriel to fall in with his plans, because they weren't the type to settle down at all. He didn't even allow himself to consider his wildest card, Jack. His own personal one-eyed Jack, wild as a March hare and bent on self-destruction.

There was nothing he could do about it now. The wheels of destiny had been put into motion long ago.

He wondered what his boys would think if they knew he was in France, in this damned Knights Templar's house—a beautiful structure, really, a history buff's timepiece—solely because their mother wasn't far from here, just a couple hours away, hidden away in a valley in France.

He knew where she was, and he'd laid eyes on her briefly. Though older, she looked the same to him, somehow more beautiful. He excused his spying, telling himself that it was normal to make certain the only woman he'd ever loved was happy. That she was well taken care of.

It was no sin to want the mother of his fine boys to be happy and to have everything she needed.

He wished she needed him, but he'd flattened that out of her long ago. He simply yearned for the time to tell his boys that life was short, that men by nature were selfish creatures who would be happier if they took the time to learn the secrets of the female heart, but he doubted it was a lesson they'd take kindly coming from him.

He couldn't solve Dane's issue, though he'd given it a shot, because his third son was the proverbial rolling stone. He understood now that the weight of a moving stone overruled everything in its path—it was not easily halted. So he bent his head to thinking about Pete's, his second son's, bachelor status. Surely there was a good woman out there, a lady just right for a man who believed he had nothing valuable to lose in life.

For just a brief moment, Josiah wondered if maybe he should just be content. He had Gabriel settled with a good wife and children. A man couldn't make decisions for his children, after all. His life was a study in decisions that had gone wrong.

But he was a father. That was all he had left to call himself. When he stood at the pearly gates, he wanted to at least be able to say, "Until my very last breath, I tried to be a good father."

Whether or not his sons would agree with that, he

couldn't answer. But he did know that a father went out fighting for his family.

And who could know? They didn't hand out redemption at the pearly gates.

Maybe, just maybe, there was a reward for effort.

DANE WAS WELL AWARE OF HIS father's plan. What he failed to understand was what was on his brother's mind. Why did Pete have such a problem with the form of entertainment Dane had selected for tomorrow? "So what's your beef with a rodeo? Some of the world's greatest fun?"

"Because it won't be fun," Pete said. He sat on a small stool and diligently polished some tack. "I hate bad ideas. I dislike poor planning."

Dane frowned. "It was no more spur-of-the-moment than us all running out for hot chocolate and a walk around town."

Pete set the tack down, glaring at his brother. "Well, we'll know tomorrow, won't we?"

"I don't know. Will we?" Dane hated his brother's mysterious issue. "Look, if you don't want to come with us, stay home."

"I could, but…three's a crowd."

"And four is…?"

"Just right." Pete nodded. "Someone needs to watch the children."

Dane raised his brows, some jealousy steaming his gut. "You're raising your hand for babysitting?"

Pete shrugged. "They're pretty cool little babies."

Dane sat opposite his brother, wondering why he chafed so at his brother's interest in Suzy's children. "Why don't we just take the group somewhere else?"

"Because you've already invoked the magic of rodeo, and anything else would be a disappointment." Pete's mouth turned down. "But we don't go until after twelve."

"What is your problem?" Dane demanded, and then the lightbulb went on. "Jack's riding!"

Pete shrugged.

"He is, isn't he?"

"Guess we'll find out," Pete said, a little sullenly.

"How do you know he is?" Dane asked, completely ignoring his brother's sour expression.

"Someone sent me a text that Jack had entered. Sure enough, he has. I checked with a buddy who's riding, and he said Jack's name was in the draw."

"Why wouldn't you want to see him?" Dane thought it'd be great to see his brother again.

"Because he doesn't want to see us," Pete snapped. "Didn't you get the hint when he was in the hospital last summer?"

Dane blinked. "Apparently not."

"He's never coming back. You can bank on that, and Pop can just get over it. This happy family gathering he's cooked up is only going to go so far." Pete shook his head. "Jack doesn't care about money, not Pop's, anyway."

"He's going to be within miles," Dane murmured, "and he won't even swing by the ranch?"

"Nope," Pete said, "why should he? This isn't his home, any more than it is yours or mine. Unlike Jack, we're here for the money." He sighed, not sounding happy about it.

"Yeah." But his plan felt like it was slipping away, thanks to Suzy. She, too, was on the ranch for money, and yet, she had so much affection for Pop that he knew she was also here because she wanted to be. He didn't, and Pete didn't, either. "I'm going to talk to Jack."

"Suit yourself."

Dane's nostrils flared. "That night was not my fault. It wasn't anyone's fault. It just happened. It's no reason for him to not want to be on speaking terms with his own brothers."

"Okay," Pete said, "but Pop told him he was trouble. Told him he would never amount to anything, and he wasn't going to drag us down with him. How do you expect Jack to feel?"

Like crap, which is how he would have felt. "I think we should overcome the old man's spirit by welcoming Jack back into the fold."

"While you take the old man's money," Pete said, annoyed, and Dane grinned.

"Be a jackass kind of thing to do, wouldn't it? Something the old man himself would do? Take the money and run?"

Pete looked at him. "The assignment was that we all live under this roof and learn to be a family."

"What better way to be a family than to bring back

the prodigal son for the even more prodigal father?"
Dane asked. "All we can do is give it a shot."

"All right, Ranger," Pete finally said after reflecting
for a moment. "One shot. And that's all we're loading
into the family firearm. Deal?"

"Deal," Dane said, satisfied that the strained family
relations would finally receive a bandage, no matter
how small.

Chapter Six

Early the next morning, before the sun was even warming the cold ground, Suzy packed her toddlers into Cricket's car. "This is going to be fun, girls."

Dane peered into the other side of her car. "There's plenty of room in my truck."

"We'll follow," Cricket said, and Suzy nodded. "You guys may want to stay later than we can—nap time can come quickly—and besides, car seats take up more room than you realize." Dane wasn't used to packing for twins; he didn't have any idea how much gear had to go along with two active young children. Anyway, she felt safer emotionally this way. If at any time the girls were cranky, she and Cricket could leave. Should Dane get tired of the busy antics of toddlers, she could put the girls in the car and say goodbye before hard feelings developed. After all, they were already living under one roof—it was best to keep matters as separate as possible, and very, very professional.

"You're definitely keeping that man in wait mode," Cricket said as they strapped themselves into her car.

"No, I'm not," Suzy said. "I'm keeping a smart amount of distance between us. Wise is the woman who doesn't mix business and pleasure."

"I respect that," Cricket said. "Just as long as you have a plan."

"I do. Put money in the bank, pay my bills, and know that I've done my job well. That's the plan."

"So will you go back to work at the hospital after the year of employment at the ranch is up?"

Cricket turned onto the main road, and Suzy watched the cold, tree-rich landscape rush by as they followed Dane's truck. She could smell crispness in the air, feel winter's chill seeping into her boots despite the car heater. "I plan to. The girls' medical insurance is covered for now under an extension plan I bought, but I'll want something more affordable soon enough. And I don't want to fall behind in the job market."

"And if Mr. Morgan wants you to stay on?"

Suzy shook her head. "My understanding is that once the year is up, and the brothers are no longer at the ranch, Mr. Morgan may sell it."

"Really?"

"He just kept it for his sons," Suzy said softly, "but they don't know that. In fact, I think he's already had several offers he's pondering."

"He wouldn't give first right of refusal to his sons?"

"I don't know," Suzy said, thinking of Mr. Morgan's

medical condition. She was pretty certain he had to have a pretty tight timetable for wrapping up his considerable estates.

"What if something should happen to him before this family experiment is over?"

That was a question she, too, had contemplated. "He must have some provision in place, but I'm not aware of what it is. He told me a few things in confidence, but nothing that pertains to what he has planned for the future."

"You're doing the right thing by not letting yourself fall for Dane," Cricket said. "He'd probably never want to settle down as long as there're all these issues with his family."

"I've got plenty of issues of my own," Suzy said, "and the last thing I want to do is deal with them. However, he might be totally excited about a deacon," she teased.

"Would you believe both of those men are a bit too wild for me?" Cricket asked with a glance at Suzy. "Could you have ever guessed?"

"We're practical women," Suzy said. "Wild men are not our thing. See how easy it is to stay single?"

SUZY THOUGHT STAYING SINGLE was the easiest thing she'd ever do in her life—until she saw Priscilla Perkins make a beeline for Dane and Pete the instant they got out of the truck at the rodeo grounds.

Cricket gasped. "What is Priscilla doing here?"

"I called her. Where better to check out very fit

bachelors?" Suzy helped her daughters out of the car, standing each girl steadily on her feet. She smiled at Sandra and Nicole in their little cowgirl hats Pete had given them. "You two are so cute. We're going to have to get pictures of you with a rodeo clown or something." She refused to look Dane's way as he was accosted by the gorgeous woman. She didn't feel stirrings of jealousy; she wasn't interested in Dane.

Sure I am. Who am I kidding? I'd have to have a screw loose not to be—

"Suzy!" Priscilla exclaimed as she realized Pete and Dane were in a group with Suzy and Cricket. "How have you been, sugar?"

She gave Suzy a smack-smack kiss, and then one for Cricket. "And these must be your girls! Hello, angels," Priscilla said in a sweet voice, "I'm Miss Priscilla! What little dolls!"

Suzy smiled at her friend. "You look well, Priscilla."

"And you do, too! Especially for a woman who carried twins!" Priscilla shuddered delicately. "I don't know how you did it, darling. And you look just fine."

Cricket picked up Sandra so that Suzy could take Nicole. "Dane, would you mind showing us to our seats? Priscilla, we need to get the girls inside. It's too cold out here for them."

"Oh, of course! You just come on in here and join me and my family in our box," Priscilla said, her voice high and friendly as she ate up Dane and Pete with her lovely eyes. "We have plenty of room!"

Suzy's heart ripped a little, just a small tear, when Dane and Pete grinned at the vivacious Priscilla, who smiled up at them adoringly. But this was an excellent time to prove to herself that the kiss Dane had pressed so hungrily against her lips had meant nothing to him at all.

DANE CONSIDERED HIMSELF a student when it came to women. He prided himself on not stepping into dumb situations where ladies were concerned. As a Ranger, he'd broken up a catfight or two, so he knew the signs of female manipulation. But Pete, the big dummy, was eying Priscilla as if she were a Christmas gift waiting to be unwrapped.

This was great. It was kind of fun watching Pete get tied around a woman's finger so easily.

"Let me help you carry one of the girls." Turning to Suzy, he took Nicole from her and followed the Pete-and-Priscilla show. They all walked inside together—so far, so good, Dane thought with satisfaction.

At that moment, a gate crashed open. The audience gasped. Their group turned to look at the cowboy being flung back and forth and up and down by the bull that had rushed from the chute. Dane felt a moment of cama-raderie for the cowboy—until he realized it was Jack. Caught by the spectacle, he could only stare as he watched his brother flail wildly on the bull determined to get rid of him. The bull wheeled around, and Dane saw that Jack had no intention of getting bucked off. It was him and the bull locked in an epic struggle of domination. Sweat broke out along Dane's upper lip as he re-membered the night Jack had been so badly hurt. In a split second he realized he'd never forgiven himself for not standing up to Pop about sneaking out to watch Jack ride. He'd wanted Jack to win the buckle, win it all—and even back then he'd known he would always sneak out to watch Jack. In his eyes, Jack was a hero, big brother who thumbed his nose at life, living it his way.

The buzzer sounded and Jack jumped off, grabbing his black hat from a clown. Another clown headed the bull off toward the gate, but at the last second, it turned for one last jab at Jack.

Jack never moved. He held his ground, staring down the bull until the last second. Then Jack jumped up onto the rail. This time the clowns were successful at shooing the bull away from another encore. Dane's breath left him in a pained rush.

"Wow," Cricket said, "I never saw anything like that in my life!"

She'd seen lots of rodeos, no doubt, so she could only be talking about Jack, and the way he'd hung on, cheating the bull of his victory. Dane watched as Cricket stepped closer to the rail, her gaze caught by Jack, who sat calmly dusting off his hat. After a moment, he glanced up, spying Cricket. A slow grin spread over Jack's face—until he realized Cricket wasn't alone, and that she was, in fact, surrounded by his own brothers.

Then he melted into the breezeway.

Dane realized Jack had never glanced up when the

announcer called his score. Once he'd beaten the bull, he was done.

"He's gone," Pete said. "We'll not see him again today."

Cricket whirled. "Who was it?"

"Our brother," Dane said tightly. "The best one."

But he knew Pete was right. Jack was gone.

"This family experiment isn't going to work," he told Pete. "We weren't meant to be a functioning family unit."

"I know," Pete said. "Come on. Let's get in Priscilla's box."

"Dane?" Suzy's voice came to him, shifting the blur of anger and guilt he felt. "Are you all right?"

"I'm fine," he said, holding Suzy's daughter tighter in his arms.

"That was cool to get to see your brother ride," Suzy said. "A moment later and we would have missed him." She followed him up into an enclosed seating area and he helped her set the children carefully on the long plank seats.

"Yeah, cool," he said. His mind was buzzing. What was it that drove them, all of the brothers, to run from their feelings for Pop? Why not just dig in their heels, ride the bull of fate until all the bad memories just wore away? Wasn't that what forgiveness was all about?

"Suzy," he said suddenly, "let me get you some popcorn. Cricket, can you watch the girls for a minute?"

Cricket nodded, and Priscilla said, "I'll help, too," and that made Pete light up. Quite the love triangle, Dane thought, but it didn't matter, because he had other plans than participating in the useless fairy tale of romantic love. "Suzy," he said as they walked down the stairs again, "I've got a business proposition for you." He halted in the breezeway and she looked up at him curiously.

"Business proposition?" she repeated.

He told his heart to quit thundering—business deals were conducted every day and this was the only way to get to Mexico and the land of gentle palm trees without being Pop's lackey. Pop didn't get it, anyway—his dream was never going to happen. "Yes. This one's pretty simple as business propositions go." He took a deep breath, shook his head to clear it, checked his conscience for guilt—none—and bit the proverbial bullet.

"If you marry me for one year," he said, "I'll split my inheritance with you."

Chapter Seven

Suzy stared up at Dane, wondering if he was having some type of meltdown after seeing his brother. It was the only thing she could think of that would make him utter such a far-fetched proposal. Coldness tinged his words, letting her know that this was a man who was running from something. "Dane, you don't want to marry me."

"I don't want to marry anyone," he said, "but the truth is, I need you, Suzy."

She shook her head. "You don't need anyone."

He put his hand on her arm for just a split second, warming her skin. "I do need you. You're the woman my father wanted me to marry. I'm simply falling in with his plan like a good soldier."

"You don't believe that," she said. "Your father is many things, but a matchmaker isn't one of them."

"Don't kid yourself. He had this all planned. At this point, I think he's a saint for giving me a way out."

"I don't understand." She really didn't. He had a wild look in his eyes—the same expression his brother Jack had worn when he rode the bull—and she had the feeling that this man, this Dane Morgan, was the same man who'd stolen a kiss from her.

"It's complicated. But if I marry you, I'll get my money. And I need to do that so that I can get out of here for good."

That certainly wasn't the marriage proposal she'd dreamed of receiving. Suzy wrinkled her nose. "As much as I'd like to help you, I don't want to marry you. Something tells me it would be a very bad idea, and I try to avoid bad ideas."

"Neither of us is a fan of getting hitched. That's why we're perfect for each other," he pointed out.

But Suzy wasn't so sure. "We're not perfect for each other." She began walking down the breezeway to break the spell between them. "Believe me, I'd love to have the money, but not that badly."

Catching her hand, he spun her toward him, ignoring the passersby who briefly stared at them. "Then consider what having my last name might mean to your daughters."

That was a cruel twist—one that went to the heart of the regret she held inside her. Of course she wanted Sandra and Nicole to have a father's last name. But lots of children didn't have the perfect family life, and she'd made peace with the fact that her girls would have to learn to be proud of being raised by a single mother. People in the town of Union Junction knew she was a good person, so she'd put the worry out of her mind.

Or so she'd thought, until Dane dangled her most secret desire in front of her like a golden key. She lifted her chin, pulled her hand from his. "Listen, buster, I don't know you well enough for you to presume such a personal conversation with me," she said bravely. "Leave my daughters out of this. Your problem is your own. I'm sorry I can't help." She waited, her heart thundering, knowing that if she turned and walked away again, he'd simply catch her hand one more time—and this time, she might say yes.

She did want to say yes. She wanted what he offered.

Yet something warned her that there was a baited hook inside the shimmering waters of the proposal he offered.

"I should have asked you more romantically," he said, "but I'm not a very romantic guy, first off, and second, I'm trying to live more in the moment these days."

She shook her head. "It doesn't matter. I wouldn't have said yes if you'd had a truck full of roses."

"I'm not asking you to hang with me for the long haul. Just a year," he said. "Only three hundred sixty-three days, actually. There's no downside to this for you."

"I beg to differ," she said coolly. "It would be cheating your father. And I'm not going to do that."

"Cheating my father?"

She nodded. "Josiah has been very good to me and my girls. He's given us a home and employment and college money. You can't know how much that means to me." She hesitated, then decided to be completely honest. "My parents don't want anything to do with my girls. Perhaps knowing that, you can understand how much it means to have your father's total acceptance and even affection for my children. So you see," she said, softening her voice, "I really couldn't participate in scamming your dad."

For a moment, Dane stared at her, shaking his head, she thought, in amazement or consternation, or perhaps it was genuine puzzlement. Maybe he simply couldn't figure out why she felt such loyalty to Mr. Morgan.

"You'll get it all figured out one day, Dane. The right answer will come to you. In the meantime, let's get you that popcorn and water for the girls."

He blinked, following her quite a bit more docilely than she'd expected. "They can't have popcorn?"

"I've got animal crackers in my purse I'm going to give them."

He stopped her again. "Why did you come with me?"

Because I wanted to. I wanted to know why your face was frozen with unhappiness. Now I know—but I wish I didn't.

When she didn't reply, a loose, slow grin spread over his face. "You like me, Suzy Winterstone," he said with a wink, "even if you deny it."

She rolled her eyes. "I won't deny it, I won't admit it, I don't even care what you think. You are just what your father said—an arrogant ass."

Dane tugged her blond hair gently and grinned.

Suzy's breath caught as the sexy man touched her, then she pushed her darkest secret deeper inside her.

She might like him, but there would never be anything between them.

"WHAT WAS GOING ON WITH YOU two out there?" Pete demanded. "You took forever, so I came to see what the holdup was before the girls started crying for their mother, and you and Suzy were standing out there whispering like naughty children."

Dane scooted in next to his brother, noticing that the suddenly silent Priscilla and the stone-quiet Cricket were seated in front of them with Suzy's children. He felt as if he wasn't part of the girls' club, and he sort of wished he was. He wondered if Suzy would tell her friends about his proposal—he hoped she would so that they could convince her that marrying him was a great idea. "We had some things to settle. Remember, she is the housekeeper."

"Oh. So did you tell her how shiny you want the toaster to be? Did you explain what kind of potpourri you prefer in the house?" Dane stared at him. "Don't kid me. The two of you were jabbering away like your lives depended upon it."

"So?" Dane stuffed some popcorn into his mouth and glanced around to make sure everyone had their treats. "Truth is, I asked her to marry me."

"Yeah, right," Pete said. "Don't think so, bro. She'd have taken your head off."

"You think?" She hadn't, and Dane felt strangely warmed by that.

"Yup. 'Cause she's got a thing for me."

Dane turned to peer at Pete suspiciously. "She might have a thing, but I doubt it's for you."

Pete shrugged. "It's true."

Dane ate some more popcorn, considering whether his brother was a liar or a great con man or just plain dumb to think Dane would believe such a tale. Why were all of his brothers so ornery?

He didn't have to ponder that hard; it was in the family tree. "Well, even if that's true, you'll just have to forget about her and pick someone else to fantasize about, like Priscilla or Cricket." He said their names softly so the ladies wouldn't overhear—odds were pretty good they wouldn't appreciate being discussed like ponies.

"Cricket's too good. I suspect Priscilla may be high-maintenance," Pete whispered.

"Your spy senses are all working today," Dane said, enjoying getting a dig in. "Pop assigned me to Suzy so you'll have to butt out."

"You're sounding pretty possessive for a guy who wants to reside in Mexico."

"You're sounding pretty weird for a spy who's probably got to be in Russia or the Congo next month."

"Actually," Pete said, "I do have to leave soon. Could be any day."

Dane blinked, annoyed by the sadness that hit him. Putting his popcorn down on the seat beside him, he couldn't make himself look at Pete. "Work?"

"Something like that."

Great. He couldn't ask for details—it was all top secret. Classified. Pete's leaving seemed somehow like a desertion. He didn't understand feeling that way, because if it were true that Pete liked Suzy, Dane should be relieved to have her all to himself. Shocked, he realized that the old man had gotten to him. It had snuck under his skin when he wasn't looking—the desire to spend time with his brothers again. A real family, just like Pop wanted. He supposed he should be grateful that he'd seen his brothers at all, but Jack didn't count, he hadn't even gotten to say hi to him. Dane had only visited a moment with Gabriel, just long enough to snag some cookies. And now Pete was off, back to Spyland where anything could happen. "Dang," Dane said, "guess I should be happy that you won't be around to annoy me."

"Guess so," Pete said.

He felt a lump in his throat. For some reason, Suzy turned around to look at him, and he couldn't swallow past the lump as she searched his face with her quick gaze. Then she turned back around to point out the next rider coming out of the chute for Sandra and Nicole. The girls got all excited, but Dane just felt sad. Maybe Pete had been right; the rodeo was a bad idea. It was a carnival of life he simply couldn't enjoy at the moment.

"Remember when you sneaked into my house in Watauga and sat down at the breakfast table?"

"Yep." Pete grinned. "The expression on your face was priceless."

"Drop in at the ranch any time," Dane said, managing to keep his tone airy. "I'm better prepared for surprises these days."

Pete chuckled. "Good man."

"Of course, you could also just call to let me know you're coming," he said, but Pete shook his head.

"It would take all the fun out of it," Pete said.

There was more to life than fun. "I want Jack to drop in one day," he said. "I'd give my million just to see him for five minutes, talk to him like the old days."

Pete nodded. "Now that would be a surprise."

"Do you think Pop knew that his scheme of being the prodigal father with the great plan was doomed?" Dane asked. "There's just no way his dream would ever happen."

"I think," Pete said, "that hope springs eternal in the human breast. Let's just remember to be better fathers if we ever get the chance."

Dane blinked. He watched as Pete's gaze slid to Sandra and Nicole, and then Suzy. Dane's hackles rose, chasing off all the warmth he'd been feeling about his brother just moments before.

There it was, that strange, territorial emotion again, something telling him that those little girls needed him to be their father in the worst way.

Convincing Suzy would be difficult, but he had a lot of experience with difficult.

"On the other hand," Pete said slowly, "I think I'll hang around just a little longer."

WHEN THEY LEFT THE RODEO a few hours later, the little girls were worn out. Pete carried Sandra, and Dane carried Nicole, and as they thanked Priscilla for sharing her box, a funny thing happened.

"You should let us return your kindness, Priscilla," Suzy said. "Come out and stay with Cricket and me at the ranch for a few days."

Dane blinked, caught by surprise. The house was certainly filling up. He glanced at Suzy, wondering if she was deliberately inviting roadblocks because of his business proposal to her. She wouldn't look at him, and he knew that the nurse was definitely meting out his medicine. He'd kissed her, he'd proposed to her and now he was going to get slipped into the psych ward.

"I'd love to!" Priscilla exclaimed. "And I happen to have some time off this week."

"What do you do?" Dane asked, curious, since Pete seemed frozen to the ground and lacking manners.

"I'm a manners coach," Priscilla said brightly. "An etiquette consultant."

Pete's jaw dropped. Dane held in a snicker. He could just see Pete telling Priscilla that he held a dangerous job that involved spying—not polite, probably—stealing— not socially acceptable and possibly even the odd assassin's role—not done in the best circles. "Great," Dane said, "come on out. The more the merrier."

He didn't really mean it, he'd like to have Suzy to himself, but if Suzy wanted to put space between him and her, he had three hundred sixty-three days to change her mind. One week of Pete and he'd probably look great by comparison. As Priscilla accepted the invitation with a smile, Dane saw Pete's rather glazed eyes light on Priscilla's lips and then move lower for just a fraction of a second.

Ah. Miss Manners and the Cold-Hearted Spy. Life was about to get interesting.

LIFE WAS SO BORING ONCE Priscilla came to stay at the ranch that Dane thought he was going to go mad. He and Pete had both moved to sleeping at the foreman's quarters far away from the fun. They'd offered to do so for the comfort of the ladies, and frankly, they didn't need to be in on every hen session, but he'd been hoping for one or two. Pete was behaving like a restless bear, and Dane hadn't seen the little girls in over twenty-four hours so he was starting to feel weird. As if he missed them. He missed the action, the constant motion of small feet.

But then he remembered how quickly and gratefully Suzy had accepted the men's offer to sleep in the guest quarters and was sorry he'd had the gentlemanly urge. "You're driving me mad," he said to Pete.

"It was a dumb idea you had, sticking us out here, a good half mile from the ladies," Pete replied.

"You said it was a great idea!"

"Well, it was dumb."

"How was I to know we'd never get invited up there?" Dane asked, stung. "I thought they'd be so happy we gave up the house that they'd invite us to dinner, maybe for a hay ride—"

"Right. I think that went out the window with your marriage proposal," Pete observed. "It feels sort of awkward around here."

Dane flung himself onto a sofa. "I don't care. I'm still ticking off days, so my goals are being met."

"Yeah?" Pete lounged across from him. "Still don't understand why I never got an assignment."

"Pop must have run out of eligible females with children."

Pete sat up. "You're right."

Dane shrugged. "So what if I am?"

"It means Pop's not matchmaking for me."

"Is that a good thing or a bad thing, in your calculation?"

Pete grinned. "It means the field is wide-open."

Dane didn't like the sound of that. "So?"

"Suzy turned you down."

"So?" Dane repeated, glaring. "She might not next time."

"And she might not turn me down at all," Pete told him.

"Oh, yes, I see. The spy and the little mother, who

will be so happy that her husband is away on dangerous assignments all the time, where he can't be reached and is no help in raising Sandra and Nicole. Don't think so."

"You're not exactly going to be available from Mexico," Pete pointed out. "I'm going up there."

"Going up where?" Dane asked.

"To the house." His brother rose and tucked his shirt into his jeans.

"We haven't been invited," Dane said. "Shouldn't we be invited?"

"You can sit around all day waiting for an engraved letter," Pete told him. "I prefer to storm the fortress."

Dane didn't want Suzy's battlements breached. "Hey," he said, hurrying after his brother. "Maybe we—"

Slowing, he examined his actions. He was acting possessive—it had been a business proposal, right? Not a marriage proposal of love and romance and lifelong dreams. He could offer the same proposal to Priscilla or Cricket, or any other woman. Further, Suzy was a grown woman. She was capable of making her own decisions and, likely, those decisions would not include him. She'd said she wasn't interested. Maybe she was interested in Pete—and if she was, it didn't mean anything to Dane.

It shouldn't, anyway.

"You coming?" Pete demanded over his shoulder.

"You go on," Dane said. "Think I'll go find some trouble."

Chapter Eight

There were some who would say that Dane was the more silent of the brothers. Gabriel was the youngest, so of course he had more personality. Raised by older brothers, he'd been pretty much left to his own devices. Plus he liked peace and harmony when he could get it.

Dane wasn't sure there was much peace and harmony to be had at the Morgan ranch.

Pete was the second son, the attention-seeker. He wanted attention, he craved action. Not much of a dedicated student, military life had been great for his sense of adventure. He couldn't wait to get away from home, and when he did, he traveled all over the world.

Like Pop.

Dane was pretty sure one could say that life at the Morgan ranch was pretty dreary for a second son seeking action.

Jack was the eldest son and, therefore, the most driven. Also the most hardheaded. He and Pop had always butted heads. Jack was going to make his own path, and he didn't care who agreed with it.

The Morgan ranch was no place for a man like Jack to twiddle his thumbs.

As the third son, Dane fell somewhere in the middle of the family hodgepodge. Happy most of the time, daring a lot of the time, independent all of the time. He could also admit to himself that he didn't like where he was in life; didn't like that he'd been ripped off by a friend, didn't like that he was turning out like Pop.

The instant he realized that, he knew exactly why he'd proposed to Suzy. He'd been looking for the easy way out of a hard dilemma. There were other ways to improve his life, make important changes.

He got into his truck and headed up the road toward Lonely Hearts Station, home of the nearby rodeo and the last place he'd seen Jack Morgan.

SUZY HAD SPENT HOURS PONDERING Dane's unorthodox proposal, and she still didn't know what to make of it. Part of her knew that he was operating out of a sense of duty to his father. Taking the easy way out, she supposed.

Part of her wished she could just give in and life could be that easy.

"So," Priscilla said, "this is a great place to live, with some minor modifications."

Cricket nodded. "It's much quieter without the Morgan men."

They laughed about that.

"And yet they're so cute, in their own ways," Cricket said. She shivered, then grabbed an afghan to wrap around herself. "Let's bake cookies. When the girls wake up, we can let them decorate."

"Oh, that will be some decorating," Suzy said. "They won't be pretty, but they'll be delicious." She glanced over at Priscilla. "Did I notice you staring at a certain bull-riding cowboy, Cricket?"

"I looked at all of them," Cricket said. "What girl in her right mind wouldn't?"

"I don't want a cowboy," Priscilla said, taking some flour and sugar out of the cupboard. "When I meet Mr. Right, I hope he's a very rich businessman. Or he definitely won't be Mr. Right. I was born to give big parties."

Suzy nodded and grabbed baking powder and vanilla from a cupboard. "I don't know what Mr. Right would be for me, but I did receive a marriage proposal this afternoon." She hadn't exactly meant to confess that, hugging the secret to her, not sure what to make of it—but it seemed safe now to share it.

"From Pete?" Cricket asked.

"Or Dane?" Priscilla asked.

Pete walked in the room. "Did I hear my name mentioned?" he asked with a grin.

The three women jumped, their gazes sliding to Suzy. Suzy shook her head at him. "If you stand around eavesdropping, you'll hear things about yourself you don't want to hear."

Pete grinned. "Like what?"

"Who knows?" Cricket shrugged at him. "If you didn't hear it, we're not sharing."

"Well," he said, his grin mischievous, "I think someone wondered if I'd asked Suzy to marry me."

The three women groaned.

"Very, very impolite," Priscilla said. "You should be ashamed."

"Why? Dane already told me. It wasn't a newsflash. Anyway, that was about him, not me. Let's talk about me." He sat in a chair, lounging, his hat pulled low, his smile wide and pleased. "Go ahead," he prompted. "Continue the conversation. Or I'll get bored and have to ask Suzy to marry me."

Suzy slapped the measuring cups onto the kitchen table. "I think I've had just enough talk about Suzy and marriage. Thank you."

"Aw," Pete said. "What else are we going to do out here in the middle of January? Play strip poker?"

Cricket shook her head. "Cowboy, maybe you better head into Union Junction for the kind of fun you're obviously hunting."

"We could play spin the bottle." Pete picked up the bottle of vanilla, giving it a spin on the table. "Must be fate. It's pointing at you, Cricket."

"Not me," Cricket said. "I have no use for wild men in my life."

Pete moved the bottle with his finger. "Ah. You, Priscilla?"

The other ladies giggled, getting drawn into his mischievousness.

"Not me," Priscilla said, "I don't kiss anybody I'm not marrying."

"Yikes," Pete said, swiftly pointing the bottle at Suzy. "Maybe Suzy."

Suzy put her hands on her hips. "I've already been kissed by your brother. I think that disqualifies me from the game."

The room went silent.

"Dane never told me that," Pete said.

"Would you expect him to?" Suzy asked.

"No," Pete said. "Is that why you turned him down? He's not a good kisser? Doesn't make your heart go pitter-patter? He could probably be trained, you know."

Suzy shook her head and grabbed the vanilla from him. "I turned down his proposal because it was dumb and he didn't mean it. He doesn't want to cheat his father. He wants to be an honest man."

"He wants that, or you do?" Pete asked, and Priscilla snapped at him with a dish towel.

"Hey, Miss Manners!" Pete exclaimed.

"You're being nosy. Go find something to do, cowboy," Priscilla said.

He looked around at the women, his gaze sheepish. "Usually women want me to hang around."

"Nah," Cricket said, "that's all in your imagination."

"Dang, tough crowd," Pete said. He put his hat on

jauntily and strode to the door. "Guess I'll go hang out in the barn."

"Where's Dane?" Suzy asked, unable to help herself.

"Don't know. Went off in a sour mood, unlike myself," he said. "I'm never in a sour mood."

"Right," Suzy said, "because you're the life of the party."

"If you don't be nice," he told her, "I'm not going to ask you to marry me." He ducked when a ball of cookie dough sailed past his head. "Okay!" he said, laughing. "Call me when they're golden brown."

He left, whistling.

Suzy shook her head and went back to mixing dough. Cricket and Priscilla glanced at each other.

"What would you say if Pete asked you to marry him?" Priscilla asked.

"He was teasing, trying to get my goat," Suzy said, not even looking up. "The man is an ape, forget about it. They're both apes."

"Yeah, but they're cute apes," Cricket said, as Priscilla nodded enthusiastically.

"Cute is for puppies. They grow up and then you've got an untrained dog on your hands, if you're not careful," Suzy said. "Preheat the oven, would you, Priscilla? I mean, what would we really do with a Morgan man? Any of us?"

"Die happy?" Priscilla asked.

"Have hours and hours of endless kissing," Cricket said dreamily, and Suzy nearly dropped her cookie cutter. The thought was tempting. She knew how good the kisses were...hours and hours of them wouldn't exactly be torture.

"I don't know," Suzy said. "They have issues. Sooner or later, issues tend to get in the way of things."

"So you're saying they're not marriage material? More like friends-with-benefits material?" Priscilla asked.

Suzy glared at her. "How would I know? I've had one serious boyfriend in my life. I'm trying not to make that mistake again."

Cricket transferred the snowman-shaped cookies onto a foil-lined cookie sheet. "Take him up on his offer, Suzy."

"Who?" Suzy glanced up.

"Dane."

Priscilla and Cricket were staring at her oddly. Suzy hesitated. "Okay, girls, stay out of the cooking sherry. There's not going to be a wedding around here, at least not one where I'm the bride." She wouldn't admit it, but Dane's proposal had stayed on her mind, playing over and over.

"There's no disadvantage to saying yes," Priscilla said, and Suzy glared.

"There is. It would be dishonest."

"It would be fun," Cricket said.

"You're a deacon. How can you be for something that's not forever?" Suzy asked. "That has a guaranteed ending?"

"Stranger things have happened," Cricket said.

"That would be very strange indeed," Suzy agreed.

Priscilla wiped up some flour with a sponge. "I wouldn't call marrying Dane an act of desperation."

"Neither of you would accept his proposal," Suzy said.

Cricket nodded. "That's true," she said. "I couldn't marry someone who had proposed to one of my dearest friends."

"Me, either," Priscilla said piously, but Suzy was pretty sure Miss Manners and the deacon were telling wee fibs to themselves.

"It doesn't matter. I'm happy just the way I am." It was mostly the truth.

"Good," Cricket said. "That was all I needed to hear you say." She pulled out a drawer to look for a pot holder. A brown envelope fell out, scattering two letters to the floor. "Oops," Cricket said, bending to scoop them up. She looked at one, then the other. "These are addressed to Pete and Jack," Cricket said, stuffing both the letters back into the larger envelope.

"Mr. Morgan hasn't been here since June," Suzy said. "Was it his handwriting?"

"I wouldn't know his handwriting," Cricket replied.

"I would. Let me see. If it's something important, Pete should know."

Cricket held the brown envelope to her. "As a deacon, I should probably safeguard us against snooping."

"As an etiquette expert, I should caution us against breaches of inappropriate happenstance," Priscilla said.

"I'll just hold up the outside so Suzy can see," Cricket said, fishing one letter out so Suzy could glance at the handwriting.

"It's Mr. Morgan's," she said. "I wonder why he

didn't ask me to make sure the men got them since I'm working here."

"Maybe he forgot," Priscilla said reasonably. "Or he wasn't expecting them to be here when you were."

Pete burst through the front door. "Are the cookies ready?" He appeared in the kitchen doorway. "Notice I loudly announced my presence this time. I don't want any more cookie dough hurled at me."

"Good. You can have this instead," Cricket said, handing him the letter with his name on it.

"Did you girls write me a love letter?" he asked, teasing. The smile slipped from his face as he saw how serious the women were. "Hey, I know I'm a little less refined than you might prefer, but I swear, for a cookie or two I can change."

"It's from your father," Suzy said, and Pete went suddenly still, the mask of cold he'd worn when she first met him slipping back over his face.

He looked at all of them, before cramming it into his shirt pocket. "What's that?"

Suzy glanced at the final letter Cricket held. "It's for your brother Jack."

"Let me have it," Pete said.

Cricket handed it to him silently.

Opening it, he scanned it, then left without saying goodbye or taking a warm cookie from the tray.

Chapter Nine

Dane had looked everywhere for Jack, but it seemed his brother had left Lonely Hearts Station right after the bull ride. Right after he'd seen his family. The trip into town wasn't completely wasted, though, because Dane had had time to think about Suzy, and he liked thinking about her.

He planned to change her mind. Maybe it wasn't heroic to try to outplay Pop, but it couldn't hurt to try. And he was still playing within the rules of the game. Pop was the one who had hired Suzy, after all, and Suzy had brought Cricket and Priscilla in to safeguard her reputation. Suzy had a point—it really wasn't appropriate for her to stay in a house of men unchaperoned.

If Suzy did agree to marry him, he'd be able to give Sandra and Nicole his name and he felt pretty good about that. He'd become very attached to those little girls. This surprised him because he never once had envisioned himself with children; in fact, he could see himself making as much of a mess of parenting as Pop.

As much as he might want to imitate his father's business success, Dane knew he'd try hard to be a better father than Pop ever was.

Sandra and Nicole seemed to like him. And he liked them. Dane considered that as he pulled into the Morgan ranch drive. Maybe he just got along better with females than with men.

He walked into the house, smelling baked cookies. Now if that didn't make a house a home, nothing would. "Mmm!" he said loudly to announce his presence. "Something smells good!"

Cricket poked her head out of the kitchen. "Come poach a cookie or two."

"Yes, ma'am." He strolled into the kitchen and was pleased to see Suzy dressed in a pretty pink apron with red hearts on it. "Hello, Priscilla," he said. "Hi, Suzy."

Suzy gave him the briefest of greetings. That didn't bode well for him—clearly she hadn't been impressed by his impromptu proposal. Well, he'd had time to think things over, plan his next move. He needed to show her some romance—she said she wouldn't be moved by a truck full of roses, but he suspected her resolve would weaken if he put in a bit more effort.

If her ex had run off on her, she'd never known romance. That was his conclusion, and he aimed to test his theory tonight.

It would require Cricket's and Priscilla's help, however. "Good cookie," he said, biting into a frosted snowman. "I like having women in my kitchen."

"You know, cowboy," Priscilla said, "you may be cute, but I'm not sure you're all that bright."

"However," Cricket said, going over to pat his biceps, as if she was flirting with him—and he knew she most definitely wasn't so something was up, "he's more than cute enough to babysit our sweet angels."

Suzy glanced up. "Oh, no, I don't think so, Cricket."

"Sure," Cricket said smoothly. "Cute and smart enough for little girls who are nearly two, aren't you, Dane?"

"Why? What's up?" He wondered if that meant he might get some alone time with Suzy, which he badly needed. He wanted to press his case with her, and he needed one-on-one time to do that. A man couldn't turn on the romance with all these women in his house—although the eats were pretty good. He snagged another cookie. "There's probably someone in Union Junction who babysits, if you really need help, Suzy."

"Nope," Cricket said. "We have our own built-in baby bodyguard. And you'll do just fine while we go pick out drape fabric. We aren't crazy about the fabric your dad chose."

Dane began to realize that the ladies were serious. He was attached to Sandra and Nicole, but he wasn't certain he was cut out to babysit. It would be a way to find out if he had any fathering proclivities, though.

"That's a fabulous idea, Cricket." Priscilla took off her apron. "Dane, do you mind if we leave this mess here for you to clean up? The little girls should be done with their naps about the time you're finished. Come on,

Suzy," she said, tugging at the tie on the back of Suzy's apron. "There's probably only a couple of hours left until the fabric store closes, and we need to measure those casements."

"I can help measure," Dane said hopefully, trying to earn his way out of the babysitting job. "We could all go to the fabric store."

Suzy shook her head. "The last place a man should probably ever go is the fabric store. All the choices would make your head spin."

"Correct as that may be," Dane said, "won't taking care of tiny, busy kiddies make my head spin?"

"Definitely," Suzy said, smiling up at him. Finally! "And by the way, we gave Pete a letter we found in a kitchen drawer. Two, actually, but one was addressed to Jack. They were from your father."

"Letters from my father?" Dane asked. "Anything for me?"

"This isn't a post office. It was just a chance find in the pot holder drawer, of all places. Don't know how they got stuck in there." Suzy put away her apron. "One letter for Pete, one for Jack. He read Jack's and then he left. He didn't even take a cookie with him."

"Did Pete say when he'd be back?"

"No," Suzy said. "We're making dinner, so I assumed he'd be back for that. You Morgan men seem happiest when your stomachs are full."

"This is true," Dane said, but he had the feeling it would be awhile before he was happy again.

"I'M NOT SURE ABOUT LEAVING Dane with the girls," Suzy said ten minutes later as the women drove away from the Morgan ranch.

"No worries," Cricket said. "He'll enjoy trying on fathering duties."

"It'll be good for him," Priscilla said. "This way, all the skeletons are out of the closet."

"What skeletons?" Suzy asked.

"You know. The ones where he isn't sure what he's getting himself into, whether he'd be a good father or not—all that stuff men worry about." Priscilla sounded very practical about the whole matter.

Suzy shook her head as she turned onto the main road into town. "What do you mean, what he's getting himself into?"

"With the marriage proposal," Cricket said. "Now he'll know if he's really cut out for the job. One afternoon with a couple of kids can tell a man almost everything about himself he needs to know. Sometimes five minutes will do the trick. When I counsel couples, you'd be surprised how many men realize they can't handle—"

"Wait," Suzy said, "I don't care whether Dane can handle being a father or not. He's not going to be a father to my girls." She glanced over at Cricket who sat in the seat next to her. "Is that what this is all about? You two cooked up a babysitting job so that Dane could try on fathering?"

"It made sense to us," Priscilla said.

"After today, we'll know if he's a man who's honest

with himself. You know, I think the Morgan men have trouble with that. They're not terribly self-aware. At least that's what it sounds like to me," Cricket said.

"I have a good mind to turn around and go back," Suzy said. "I invited you girls out to the ranch to be my friends, share a few laughs and protect my reputation. Not audition fathers and matchmake."

"We weren't the ones who offered you a business-marriage proposal," Priscilla said. "As a business-woman, however, I think you need to give yourself forty-eight hours to think over the deal before you reject it out of hand."

"I could never cheat Mr.— Hey, look!" Suzy slowed her car down.

"That's the cowboy!" Cricket exclaimed, her voice full of awe and admiration. "Stop, stop, Suzy!"

Suzy wasn't sure if she was making the best decision, considering the tone of her dear friend and deacon's voice, but stop she did, slowing down so that Cricket could roll down the window.

"Need a ride?" Cricket asked, her tone laced with more come-hither than Suzy had ever heard from her before.

"With three hot ladies? Sure do," the cowboy said, and Suzy realized drapery fabric wasn't going to be bought today as Jack Morgan slid into the backseat.

Chapter Ten

"Where are you headed, ladies?" Jack asked.

"I think the question is, where do you want to go?" Suzy asked. "I'm Suzy Winterstone, by the way. This is my friend Priscilla Perkins and Deacon Cricket Jasper." She emphasized *deacon* because she could see Cricket making goo-goo eyes at Jack.

"Wait a second," he said to Cricket, "you're that girl from the rodeo."

Cricket nodded, stars in her eyes. "Good memory."

"Not really," he said. "I just never forget a beautiful woman."

Suzy groaned. "Can we perhaps drop you off, maybe, I don't know, at the Morgan ranch?"

He looked at her suspiciously. "Why?"

"Because you're Jack Morgan, the oldest, and hardest-to-get-hold-of Morgan. Pete and Dane have been hoping you'd swing by. In fact, we found a letter in a drawer today with your name on it," Suzy said hurriedly. "It would be no trouble to take you to the ranch for a bit." She didn't say that Mr. Morgan's ill health was an even better reason for Jack to set foot on the ranch, but by the anger now blazing in Jack's eyes, she figured she was already pushing her luck.

"I don't need a ride anymore," Jack said, starting to get out of the car, but Priscilla tugged him back.

"Or we could take you to a bar," she said, batting her eyes.

"I don't do bars," he said crossly. "I don't even drink."

"Wow," Cricket said, "and you're supposed to be such a tough guy."

"Tough guys don't drink," Jack told her. "At least they don't if they want to ride bulls as long as I have. Thanks for the offer. I'll have to pass." He got out of the car.

Cricket got out, too. "I'll go with you."

Suzy's mouth dropped open. "Cricket!"

He grinned at Cricket. "I don't have a chariot, lady, as you can see."

"I like to walk," she said resolutely.

"I've only got a couple hours until I need to be in another town," Jack said. "And besides, I sort of smell a trap."

Cricket shook her head. "I'm a deacon. I'm honest by nature and by trade. And Suzy's your brother Dane's fiancée."

Jack glanced at Suzy again. "Lucky Dane."

Suzy leaned her head out the window. "Cricket, honey, we need to get back to the ranch. Remember,

Dane is babysitting my twins, and he's probably in danger of losing his mind."

Jack laughed. "You left Dane babysitting twins?"

Suzy nodded. "He likes children. Sort of like your father," she said, trying to get Mr. Morgan into the conversation—anything to try to stir some familial feelings in Jack.

He glanced at Cricket, then slowly shook his head, like he was coming out of a fog. "Sorry, doll. It's best if I don't get sidetracked." Then he loped off down the road, catching a ride instantly with a redhead in a blue Corvette.

"Darn," Cricket said, getting back into the car. "We nearly had him."

"*You* nearly had him," Priscilla said in wonder. "I didn't know you could sweet-talk a man like that!"

"I didn't, either," Cricket said. "My knees were knocking."

Suzy felt as if they'd missed a great opportunity, but she didn't know how they could have been more successful unless they'd locked the doors and dragged Jack back to the ranch. She didn't think he was the easiest man to kidnap, even with three women in the car to butter him up. "He's never going back."

"Heart of stone," Priscilla said. "Just like a cowboy is supposed to have, I guess."

"Heart of stone," Cricket murmured. "Mine is beating like a drum."

"Oh, boy," Suzy said. "Cricket, that is a man who should wear a vest marked Broken Hearts Ahead. Do not think about him anymore. And I am not engaged to Dane! I'm of the serious opinion that Morgan men should be avoided."

"You're right," Cricket said, but the deacon looked out the window with a sigh, and so Suzy drove on to Union Junction.

ONE HOUR AFTER THE TWINS had awakened, Dane was ready to throw in the towel. The girls were darling and sweet but they were into everything, all at once, and it seemed he didn't have enough eyes in his head to see the temptations they couldn't resist. Cookies had been mashed into the carpet, shaving cream sprayed on the sofa, and—he couldn't even understand how they had found this—a broken jar of coins was spilled all over the floor. Big jar, too, probably an old pickle barrel jar, at least sixty-four ounces in size.

He had to scoot the girls away from the broken glass and the scattered coins, praying they wouldn't get cut. While he was engaged in emergency cleanup, the girls went back to the can of shaving cream, much to his chagrin.

And yet he couldn't be mad at them. Somehow, he adored their pixie faces all the more. How could anyone not love such girls after his own heart? "You girls think you're doing new things, but this is nothing. You should have seen the trouble my brothers and I could get into."

They looked at him, their fingers in their mouths, which he hoped didn't have a lot of shaving cream. He resolved to wash their hands immediately, as soon as he vacuumed up the last bits of broken glass. Nicole and Sandra were finally still and they watched him from the bottom stair with great curiosity.

"You have to wear shoes now, all the time," he said. "I don't trust my cleaning skills around tiny bare feet. Come on. Let's go upstairs and find you something to wear."

The girls went upstairs with him rather docilely—this was a new game, searching through their bags with a man and not their mother, so they patronized him with good charm. "What are these things?" he asked, holding up a ridiculously small pair of rubber Crocs from Nicole's bag. "These look safe. And they have this furry stuff inside, which will keep you warm until your mother gets home and tells me I've dressed you wrong. But at least you'll be safe and warm." He slid the Crocs onto Nicole's feet, examining them. "Not the most attractive shoes, but I can see the appeal. And glass won't get to you, best of all." He found a second pair to slide on Sandra's feet, and glanced at the bags again. "How come your mother hasn't unpacked your suitcases? Isn't she planning to stay for a while?"

Receiving no answer, he glanced into the closet. Suzy's things weren't unpacked, either. He thought about that for a moment, deciding it was none of his business.

Yet it bothered him. He wondered if she hadn't unpacked because of him. "Let's put some bows in your hair and surprise your mom," he suggested. "First we need to get the toothpaste and shaving cream out, though." He rooted around, found some little bows and brushes and sat down, wondering how he was going to manage tidying little heads full of shiny, flyaway hair.

Thirty minutes later, the girls showed no signs of their midday mischief. "Now," he said with satisfaction, "no one can say I'm not a competent babysitter. Let's go downstairs and find a proper container for all those coins before your mother returns. We'll be finding those for weeks. I don't think they even make glass pickle jars that size anymore."

The girls followed him on this new adventure, thrilled that they were getting so much attention from Dane. Babysitting was more fun than he thought it would be.

"Probably not something we should get used to," he said to the girls as he helped them down the stairs so they wouldn't trip in their little rubber shoes. "Your mother is bound to say I've done everything wrong."

He searched out a plastic rain bucket and began spilling the dimes, nickels and quarters into it. "Look at these relics, girls. These are buffalo heads and mercury heads. Pop was quite the collector, not just of houses and property but coins."

That was the thing about Pop, Dane realized. He'd been born for success. Everything he touched—even loose change—turned out to be valuable. He had the Midas touch, except with his own family.

"You know," Dane told the girls, who were enraptured by the sound of the tinkling coins, "I thought I was going to be a success like my old man. Only I wasn't going to make the mistake of being a jackass along the way. I always thought it was his business dealings that made him hard, so I was going to prove to him and myself that one could be successful without being like him." He shrugged, dusted off his hands and stood. "Maybe if I'd been a little tougher, I would have known that my partner was scamming me, huh?" He went into the kitchen, and the girls followed, watching as he washed his hands. Then he washed theirs and they didn't even protest, much to his delight. "So that was today's lesson from the school of hard knocks. Try not to forget it, okay?"

The front door opened, and Suzy flew inside.

"Hey," Dane said, "find the perfect fabric?"

She halted, her gaze searching out her children anxiously. "No," she said, then hurried to hug her daughters. "You girls look beautiful."

"Yeah. Uncle Dane is good with the beauty tricks," he said proudly, earning himself a frown from Suzy.

"We saw your brother," she said, and he glanced at her.

"Pete?"

"Jack."

Now she had Dane's complete attention. "You saw Jack?"

"We even had him in my car for about sixty seconds."

"I can't believe it." Dane shook his head.

"We did our best to lure him to the ranch, but he wasn't biting," Cricket said, coming inside with a bag of cookies and some loose tea she'd bought in Union Junction.

"We even told him about the letter Pete has for him

from your father," Priscilla said, "but he didn't seem interested at all."

"No. He wouldn't." Dane looked at Suzy. "Thanks for trying, but I'm resigned to the fact that he's never coming back."

"He's a bit crazy," Suzy said, but at the same time she thought all the men were. Her little girls were dressed up like angels and obviously completely happy to have spent some time with Dane—she'd expected all kinds of mess and drama when she returned. Dane hadn't seemed like he'd be the most organized when it came to small children. "Crazy in the sense that I think he's just rolling from town to town. He was hitching, so I guess he doesn't even have a vehicle of his own."

"Yeah. Well, whatever." Dane turned back to the sink and dried his hands. "So, no fabric?"

Suzy watched Dane's face carefully. He was upset, but he wasn't going to let on. "We'll get it next time."

Dane shrugged. "It's not my house. I don't care."

"Well. I think I'll grill some cheese sandwiches," Priscilla said brightly. "Do you think Pete will be back soon?"

"I doubt it," Dane said. "I tried reaching him on his cell phone but all I got was a recording that he'd be out of the States for the next month."

"The next month?" Priscilla looked shocked. "I thought he had to stay here for a year."

"I don't think that was his plan. He's more of a pop-in-when-you-least-expect-it kind of guy," Dane said.

"Anyway, guess I've got you ladies to myself now. All five of you. How lucky can a guy get?"

"Even luckier," Suzy said. "If your business proposition is still on the table, I'd like to accept."

Chapter Eleven

Cricket and Priscilla gasped, but Dane just stared at her. Suzy could feel her heart beating in her throat.

"Why?" he asked. "Seeing Jack change your mind?"

"I'm not sure," she said, knowing that was indeed the big motivator. "It just came to me that this is the right thing to do."

She wasn't being completely honest, but she hadn't even told Cricket and Priscilla she was going to accept Dane's offer—it seemed to have flown out of her mouth. Yet she knew it was the right decision.

"Well," Dane said, "that makes me a lucky guy."

"That's what your brother said," Cricket observed, and Priscilla nodded.

"Did he?" Dane looked at Suzy, watching her.

"Yes," Suzy said, "but he was being polite."

"I don't think polite describes Jack. I haven't seen him in years, but I remember him being more of a hell-raising, don't-give-a-dang-what-anybody-thinks person. If he said I was lucky, he meant it," Dane said, grinning from ear to ear.

"I'm not saying his approval changed my mind," Suzy said.

"I hope money won't, either," Dane said. "I don't have any, except for what my father has promised each of us, and which I have, incidentally, decided to turn down."

The three women stared at him.

"Well," Dane said, "independence is a powerful motivator. I just need to start over in my life. I can do this on my own—I was too trusting and I paid for that mistake. Just thought you should know that the parameters of the proposal have changed."

Suzy put her hands on her hips. "Not for me," she said. "I wasn't marrying you for money. Mr. Morgan pays me quite well. You were marrying me for *your* money. I was marrying you so my girls would have a last name."

He considered that. "I'll have to think about it," he said. "Not the part about the girls, but whether I want to have a wife I can't afford."

"Oh, pish," Cricket said. "Two can live as cheaply as one, especially when neither of you is paying for this roof over your head."

"Except I won't be living here," Dane said. "There's no point. My brothers aren't here, and I don't want the money, so there's no reason to stay."

"Very mature of you," Priscilla said. "Independence in a man is attractive. Don't you agree, Suzy?"

"I don't know," Suzy said, "I'm not the one to ask

about family matters. But I have a two-bedroom house I haven't rented out yet, so technically—"

"Two bedrooms?" Dane said, brightening. "That sounds quite cozy."

Suzy looked at him with some concern. "We haven't discussed the fact that this is an in-name-only marriage."

Dane tried to look innocent, failing miserably. "I'm up for discussing sex any time you want to."

"Ha," Cricket said. "Priscilla, maybe we should take the girls for a walk so these two can decide if a merger between two entirely dissimilar people is a good thing."

"Come on, girls," Priscilla said. "Let's go look for some pecans. That wind the other night should have blown down plenty. We can make chocolate pecan pie."

"I never said you both couldn't be part of this merger," Dane said agreeably. "We could do a commune kind of thing."

Priscilla put some mittens on the little girls. "As you said, you don't have any money, and it would take money to keep Cricket and me. We're more hard-hearted than Suzy."

"Hey," Suzy said, "I'm trying to raise two children. I think money is lovely."

But Priscilla and Cricket had already left, leaving her alone with a very handsome cowboy.

"What changed your mind?" he asked.

"You were right. It was your brother. Cricket looked like she was going to jump into the backseat and eat him up. I would have thought a deacon would have better sense." Suzy blinked. Maybe she was no different than Cricket—same story, different man.

"What does that have to do with me?"

"I felt sorry for him." She tried to figure out if Dane was buying her story. "He seemed sort of lost to me. And I've decided the best way I can help your father is to tie you down for a year."

He laughed and the sound slid along her skin, tempting her. "You're going to settle me, Suzy Winterstone?"

She raised her chin. "It's my best offer."

He looked at her, his gaze suddenly resembling a wolf's. "I don't think so."

"You don't think what?" She was wading into ever deeper water, trying to read his mind.

"I don't think you're being completely honest, maybe with me, maybe with yourself, but honesty is not your strong suit at the moment." He slid a hand along her arm, which she jerked away.

"Look," she said, "my girls win if I marry you, my parents may even be slightly impressed that I'm no longer a single mother, and it will please Mr. Morgan." She gave him a cool glance. "He of all people will understand the sacrifice I'm making for the cause."

"The cause of family harmony." He leaned against the kitchen wall, taking in everything she was saying. "You need me for something."

"And I just told you. My girls, my own reputation. Don't make this harder than it is," she snapped.

He chuckled. "I'll find out in time what motivates you, Suzy W."

She remained silent, gazing at him stubbornly.

"A lot of women are motivated by money. It's okay to admit you are, too. It's a playing field I understand."

"I never said I wasn't motivated by security," she told him. "Job security is very important."

"So we're moving into a two-bedroom house," Dane said. "I like closeness."

"I'll expect you to pay your share of rent," she said.

"Of course," he replied. "I've got a bucket full of money just for that. Well, my entire net worth is now a bunch of old coins in a bucket, but it'll do for the rainy day theory."

She shook her head. "What happened to the pickle jar? Isn't that Mr. Morgan's?"

"Mr. Morgan happens to be out at the moment. And I, uh, broke the jar, but since I cleaned up all the glass, I'm keeping the change." He grinned at her rakishly. "I'll call it my babysitting fund."

"You did seem to be a relatively decent babysitter," she said reluctantly. "I think the girls like you."

"Those little girls like me almost as much as their mother does," Dane said. "I suspect you'll be just as lucky for me as they are."

Suzy moved to walk past him, but he caught her hand, pulling her up against him. "Say you want wedding vows so you can kiss me again," he said huskily. "I think about kissing you often."

She stepped past him. "I told you, I'm marrying you to make an honest man of you," she said, walking away.

"Can't be done, I fear," he called after her.

"Maybe not," she murmured so that he couldn't hear, "but my girls are going to have a family. I'm not going to end up like your brother Jack."

FORGIVENESS MATTERED TO DANE more than he was willing to admit. He wasn't going to have a gabfest over it, cleanse his soul by confession, but the family condition was starting to get to him. Maybe it was seeing how happy Gabriel was now that he'd made amends with Pop. His gaze slid to the little fair-haired tots climbing over Suzy's lap and wondered how much his latent feelings of contrition had to do with Suzy's children.

Damn Pop, anyway.

The old man would grin if he could see Dane sitting around worrying like a girl over the past. Nothing could be changed, anyway. And he'd already improved matters. Suzy had decided to marry him, hadn't she, and that alone would make him a better man.

Maybe. He had the notion that he was screwing everything up despite his best efforts to fix things. That sneaking suspicion just wouldn't leave him alone, either.

"I'll perform the ceremony, if you two like," Cricket said. "It would be my pleasure."

"Do you have a problem with that, Dane?" Suzy asked.

Did he? He looked into her eyes and didn't think so. He didn't know what to think. "Sounds convenient."

"I'll plan the reception," Miss Manners said.

"No reception," Dane said.

Suzy quickly added, "Thank you, Priscilla. We don't really have anyone to invite."

A sad commentary if he'd ever heard it. He noticed Suzy hadn't mentioned inviting her folks to the wedding—wasn't that sort of a bad sign? Marrying someone who had the same difficulty promoting family harmony as he did?

"All right," Priscilla said brightly, not bothered at all. "I'd love to help plan a bridal shower. Or the honeymoon. Travel plans are so much fun to make, don't you think, especially for newlyweds!"

Suzy and Dane stared at her. Honeymoon! He hadn't even considered such a thing. He nonchalantly peered at Suzy to see if she was going to protest that suggestion, as well, but Suzy sat there silently, her gaze going to her children.

So she didn't exactly abhor the thought of being alone with him...which cheered him immensely.

"Dane, I thought I heard you say something about Mexico," Priscilla said, but Suzy shook her head.

"Nothing elaborate." Suzy looked around at her friends. "This is a business deal, remember? Romance isn't required."

Dane wanted to interrupt and say that romance might not be required but he was certainly open to it. The serious look on Suzy's face kept him from trying to make light of the honeymoon idea.

"Here's a thought," Priscilla said. "Cricket and I can watch the girls after the ceremony, and you two can go out and have a nice, businesslike dinner. A seal-the-deal kind of meal. Even enemies shake hands over negotiations, don't they?" she asked sweetly.

Dane wondered whose side Priscilla was on. He glanced at Suzy, interested to see whether she would allow her girls to be watched while he took her out for a postnuptials dinner. To his surprise, Suzy seemed to be waiting on him to answer. "Suzy?" he said. "I'm up for whatever you want."

"Dinner would be all right," she said reluctantly.

"Of course, we don't mean a burger place," Cricket said hurriedly. "Someplace reasonably upscale, so that when the girls are grown, you can show them pictures of the nice restaurant where you celebrated your vows. Even though you'll be divorced by then, the girls will enjoy seeing their mother's wedding night dinner."

"Good idea," Dane said. He felt sad, though, that he wouldn't be around to see the girls admire those pictures. "So, when's the earliest we can do this?"

"Three days," Cricket said, "after you apply for a marriage license."

"And I do feel that I need to ask your father—"

"No." Suzy's quiet tone sliced off what Dane was about to say.

He blinked. "Suzy, look. I'm no stranger to family squabbles. But I'm neutral territory here. Your father can hardly object to me asking for your hand. I'm a traditional guy, and already I'm veering out of my comfort zone with a short-term marriage."

"You asked me for a short-term marriage," Suzy reminded him.

"Right. But as I said before, there's no harm in asking. It really doesn't bother me to go ask your father, even if he won't open the door for me."

"The worst Mr. Winterstone can do is say no," Priscilla said reasonably. "And then what would you do?"

"Well, I'd…" Dane looked at Suzy's worried face. "I'd tell him he was being an old donkey and missing out on the three best things in life he could be enjoying—his daughter and two sweet granddaughters."

Suzy gave him a look of gratitude, which made him feel rather important, as if he might have scored serious points.

"Dane, we all know this is a temporary solution. It's very sweet of you to offer, but no thank you. You have to understand that my situation is very different from yours. My family basically cut off ties with me. Your father wants you back in his life desperately. He just doesn't know how best to make that happen."

He shrugged. "Let's deal with applying for a marriage license. I suppose we go to the Union Junction courthouse for that?"

Cricket nodded. "Why don't you two go do that while we watch the girls?"

Suzy smiled. "Thank you."

"Suzy, quit acting like we're doing you a favor," Priscilla said. "Your little girls are awesome."

"Still, it is a favor, and I owe you big-time." Suzy took a deep breath. "I'm ready whenever you are, Dane."

He felt like something was lacking, something fundamental. This was a special time, wasn't it? Getting a marriage license was the first step in a long road they'd take together. He felt sentimental about the journey, but maybe that was because he'd never seen himself married and now it was happening, goodbye freedom and all that.

Except "goodbye freedom" wasn't as bad as it sounded. He was looking forward to marrying Suzy. As much as he probably shouldn't be sentimental about their business deal, he was.

Was that a bad sign? He glanced at his little bride's serious face and wondered just how much he might be kidding himself.

DANE HELPED SUZY INTO HIS truck and they headed toward Union Junction without saying much to each other beyond pleasantries. Suzy tried to tell herself how practical she was being. Marrying Dane was a great idea, both for the girls and for her. It was a win-win situation for Dane, as well, because he could get what he wanted, which was his money, even though he claimed he wasn't going to accept it. She doubted he really felt that way; right now, he was angry with his father and feeling as if he had to do what he was doing, which was marry a woman his father had installed in his house to lure him to the altar. Dane was being very nice about it, but no man married a woman he'd kissed once and didn't love unless there was a fat paycheck involved. Suzy figured Dane didn't want to live on his "pickle fund" forever, and would elect to take the money from his father after all.

"Good thing I changed my mind about Pop's money," Dane said cheerfully, "or this excursion would be a drudge."

She wrinkled her nose. "It is a drudge, whether or not you accept money to do it."

"Now that does not sound like a happy bride," Dane said, "and I think I prefer my bride happy."

"Well," Suzy said, "it's hard to act like a giddy bride when we're not in love."

"That's something money cannot buy," Dane agreed. "I think I prefer marriage more cut-and-dried, though. It's exciting enough like this."

"You may be a bit of a romantic," Suzy said, "which surprises me a little, because I see you as being totally unlike your father."

"Nah," Dane said. "I'm sure the apple doesn't fall far from the tree." He offered her a brief smile. "Much to my chagrin, I probably have some of the old man's traits."

"Maybe." Suzy looked out the window, feeling nervous. "Did you call him?"

"No. Why should I?" He sounded surprised.

"Same reason you wanted to go see my father. To share the good news."

"I figure Pop doesn't need any good news. He's over

there in France, enjoying the good food and the retirement living."

"I think he would want to know." Suzy knew full well that Mr. Morgan would be ecstatic, and she wondered if there was another reason Dane was unwilling to tell him.

"I'll tell him when I'm ready."

"Okay." It was his family. She wasn't going to worry about how he handled Mr. Morgan. Her part was done. From now on, all she had to worry about was going over to the Morgan ranch and making sure it stayed clean, festive and homey. Hang draperies…she shook her head. "You know how I said we could live in my house?"

He nodded. "I'm looking forward to getting off the ranch."

"Technically, though, my contract with your father says I'm supposed to stay at the ranch to give it a lived-in feeling," Suzy said. "I don't want to have to turn in my resignation, but I'm pretty sure that me not living at the ranch is in conflict with the idea of a live-in housekeeper."

"Now that you mention it," Dane said, "you may have a point. You'll have to quit your job."

"I'm not quitting my job," Suzy said. "I have to be employed. You might be okay with unemployment, but I've got two little girls to feed."

"Hey," Dane said, "I never said I wasn't going to work."

"What you do doesn't concern me," Suzy said. "I'm not expecting you to take care of me and my girls."

"Suzy Winterstone, I'm afraid my idea of marriage and your idea of marriage may not be the same."

"Marriage is a contract," Suzy said. "I keep all my contracts to the letter."

"Well, then, write this into our contract," Dane said. "I most definitely plan on taking care of you and your girls for the next year just like you were my real wife."

Chapter Twelve

Dane was stubborn. It was in his family genes, and he was becoming more proud of it by the day. He meant every word he said to Suzy about taking care of her—and the more he felt her shrink away from a real commitment to him, the more he found himself digging in his heels.

"Maybe we should discuss this marriage a bit more," Suzy said, her voice faint.

"We could talk it to death," he said, "but I'm still going to be a real husband to you."

He thought she went a little pale, and then realized she was probably thinking he meant sex. The considerate side of him started to correct her assumption, but then the Morgan side of him jumped up and yelled in his ear, *Who are you kidding? Of course you want to make love to this woman!*

So he didn't say anything, just enjoyed watching her fidget. "You went very quiet on me, Suzy."

"I think you should know something about me," she said.

"Lay it on me." He figured she was going to tell him the real reason her parents didn't want to see their own grandchildren.

But what she said instead was, "I'm not good in bed."

His jaw sagged. He didn't know how to reply to that.

"I just thought you should know," she said hurriedly, "if you really mean to be a real husband to me."

"Well, hell," he said, not sure where he was going with that, but grasping, grasping for the right words to say. "How does someone be not good in bed?"

"I don't know," she said. "I'm not a very passionate person."

He started laughing. "Nah. Can't be."

"Why?" she demanded. "And quit laughing. It's not funny in the least. The worst thing a woman can ever be is bad in bed."

"It's not too good for the guy, either." He wiped the grin off his face, however, trying to be sensitive to her feelings. "We'll worry about grading the marital relations later, okay?" He thought she was sexier than ever when she was all worried about her sensuality. She oozed schoolgirl innocence and he wanted to ravish her this minute.

She raised her chin. "I can tell you're not paying attention to me."

"Oh, Suzy," he said, very serious now, "you can rest assured about one thing—I am paying very close attention to everything about you."

THE MAN WAS CRAZY IF HE KNEW the truth and still wanted to be a "real husband" to her, Suzy thought crossly. He wouldn't ever be able to say he wasn't warned, and that was the most she could do. Now that she had her soul's darkest confession out of the way, Suzy began to relax. It was only a year, after all. Even a man as handsome and downright sexy as Dane Morgan could stand one year of not-so-great sex.

At least she hoped he could. She would do her best to work on her problem. If he really intended to be a real husband to her, then she would do her utmost to be a real wife to him. The fail-safe on this whole thing was that both of them knew that they wouldn't have to lie to each other forever.

She had always known she would never get married because of her problem. Now it was as if Dane had lifted a great weight of doubt from her.

"Priscilla just texted me," Suzy said. "She wants to know if you want a groom's cake."

"I thought we weren't having a reception," Dane said.

"It looks like the two of them have decided to bake two cakes with the girls. One traditional wedding cake, which Priscilla says will be a white sheet cake, and then a groom's cake, which will apparently be a chocolate pecan turtle-style kind of cake since they're going out to pick up pecans."

He smiled. "Chocolate pecan cake sounds wonderful. Sure. It'll be great, especially if the cherubs are going to help with the baking."

She realized he was flattered that her friends had thought of baking him a groom's cake. Maybe all this man needed to soften him up was some thoughtfulness. "I need to call your father," she said, hating to bring it up.

"To give him your resignation?"

"No!" Suzy stared at him. "Dane, I'm not about to give up good employment. I hope your father will still allow me to be the housekeeper, even though I won't be a 'live-in.'"

"I don't know if I like having a wife who works," Dane said.

"You'll have to deal with it."

"Okay," he said, "then I'll go apply with the local law enforcement agency. I can do another year's worth of Ranger work. Or whatever serves as law around here. Once a Ranger, always a Ranger, as the saying goes."

She looked up from the text she was sending Priscilla. "That scares me."

"Really? I thought women loved a man in uniform."

"Well, I'm sure you're very handsome and all, but…doesn't your father need a lot of work done at the ranch?"

"Which doesn't pay," he reminded her, "and I need to take care of you."

"Stop saying that," Suzy said. "I'm more independent than you think."

"Hey," he said, "I can be a stay-at-home dad. That would be fun. You work, and I'll teach the girls ranch life."

Her heart slid sideway. He was charming the socks

off her, wooing her through her children. And it was working. Nothing said masculine more than a man who loved a woman's children. "It doesn't pay."

"Maybe not in coin. But I'd win lots of points with you." He grinned at her, which made her think maybe he wasn't quite as charming.

"I don't see you as stay-at-home dad material."

"But you don't want to be married to a cop."

"My ex-boyfriend is a cop," she said. "I don't have fond memories."

"I bet." He considered that for a long moment and then nodded. "All right. Stay-at-home father it is. It was my first choice, anyway."

Suzy looked out the window, smiling to herself. "You don't know what you're getting yourself into."

"You have no idea how good I am at cleaning up unexpected messes."

He was too perfect. There was something wrong here. No man wanted to take on a woman with children, especially a woman he knew had sexual issues, and promise to take care of her and be a father to her children. She searched for his motivation, but since he'd vowed to give up his million dollars, she couldn't figure out what it was Dane Morgan really wanted from their marriage.

DANE SUDDENLY HAD HIS YEAR all planned out: (1) Marry Suzy. It was a good deal for both of them; (2) Convince Pete to back him in a cattle operation. Do a little soybean farming, maybe even figure out a way to profit from all those pecan trees bordering the property. In general, become the salt of the earth his father had never been. There was enough land at the Morgan ranch to do whatever he wanted, and Pop was probably losing all kinds of tax benefits by not deducting crop taxes, etc. If he could turn this ranch into a profitable operation rather than just a piece of real estate—he would spend a year being able to train himself in business, which would be a great thing when he moved to Mexico. Experience was everything. Maybe he could even talk Jack into coming home and raising some horses. Okay, that was far-fetched, but it was a thought.

If he had to be in Texas, he might as well use his time wisely. He felt pretty good about his goals. "Here we are," he said to Suzy as he pulled up outside the courthouse. The white stone building looked as if it hadn't changed in a hundred years or more. "Last chance to back out."

Suzy looked at him, her eyes big in her face. "I'm not backing out. You're the one with wandering feet."

"I'm changing," he told her, "thanks to you."

"Don't blame it on me," she said, getting out of the truck. "You forget that I've met all of your brothers. Only one of you is able to stay in one place for long."

"I crave excitement," Dane said cheerfully, "and the past few days have brought me more adventure than I've ever had."

She shook her head. "So says the Texas Ranger."

"Family life is much more exciting than law enforcement, you know," he said, taking her elbow to guide her through the courthouse door. "I could write a book about the Morgans."

"That's what you can do to make money," Suzy said. "Write a screenplay about a father who wants his four sons to love him."

"Doesn't sound like a very exciting movie." Dane steered her toward a door that looked like a records office. "Hello," he said to the elderly woman behind the desk. "We're here to apply for a marriage license."

She looked over her glasses at him. "Suzy?"

"Hello, Mrs. Cole," she said. "Dane, this is Celie Cole."

"Hello." He shook her hand warmly. "Nice to meet you."

Celie smiled at him. "I heard from Cricket. She was checking on the marriage application process in Union Junction County."

"Cricket's getting us organized," Dane said. "She's planning our wedding."

Celie clapped her hands with genuine delight. "I assume I'll get an invitation, Suzy?" Her tone implied that the invitation should already be in the mail.

Suzy blinked, not wanting to say that no one was being invited.

"Carla, Suzy's getting married to Dane Morgan," Celie said before Suzy could stop her. A tall, thin woman came over with a friendly smile on her face.

"That's great! I bet Josiah is thrilled!" Carla gazed

at both of them benevolently. "He's always wanted a bunch of little ones out at that place of his."

"Yes," Suzy said. "But—"

"Let me give you a his-and-her shower," Celie said. "After everything Mr. Morgan has done for Union Junction, it's the very least I can do."

"Oh, by all means," Carla said. "We couldn't let a Morgan wedding go by without doing our part. Mr. Morgan has been the saving grace of this town with all his generous donations."

Dane shook his head. "Thank you, it's so thoughtful, but we just couldn't—"

"Oh, you must," Celie insisted. "I'd do anything for Josiah, as would most people in this town. Everyone's going to want to help."

Suzy glanced at Dane, not sure what to say. She didn't want to hurt the ladies' feelings, but she hadn't planned on a wedding or a shower…and yet, less than the expected fanfare would make people suspicious. To cause gossip about Mr. Morgan and his family after all Josiah had done to repair his reputation didn't seem right.

Apparently, Dane was coming to the same conclusion because he said, "We weren't planning on a large wedding, Mrs. Cole."

"That's right," Suzy said. "In fact, Cricket and Priscilla are making the cakes for us."

Celie's eyes lit up. "I would consider it my duty and a way to thank Josiah if you would allow me to host a very tiny girls-only shower, then, with homemade finger sandwiches and lemonade."

"Yes," Carla said, "we could do a very simple shower, just the girls you worked with at the hospital."

Maybe this was the easy way out. "Well, if it would be very small," Suzy said, trying to think of how devastated the ladies would be when she and Dane didn't stick their marriage out for more than a year. "Very, very simple. Nothing more than lemonade."

Celie and Carla smiled. "Well, and tea and coffee, naturally."

Suzy slowly nodded. "You're very sweet to do this."

"Nonsense," Celie said. "We're delighted to do something for Josiah. I imagine he'll be flying in for the wedding?" she asked Dane.

"We haven't exactly broken the news to him yet," Dane hedged, and Celie squealed.

"Carla, we're almost the first to know!"

"We really just decided this morning," Suzy said, and Carla nodded.

"That explains why you're not wearing an engagement ring," she said.

"We're about to go shopping," Dane said quickly. "We decided to apply for the marriage license first."

Suzy couldn't look at him. She knew he had no money, and the expense of a ring wasn't necessary when they weren't staying together.

"Well, let's get started!" Celie exclaimed, sounding as if the most prominent couple in Union Junction had just announced their impending marriage. "I'll just need your birth certificates or driver's licenses and we can get started. This is so exciting!"

Thirty minutes later, when they'd completed the paperwork, Dane could tell his new fiancée was completely rattled as they left the courthouse. Worried, he'd wondered if Suzy might bolt. He hadn't considered the fact that everybody in Union Junction knew Suzy had been unceremoniously dumped by her ex-boyfriend—and the romantic notion she'd suddenly found true love would be too much of a fairy tale for the town's ladies to resist. "Heart-pounding excitement, huh?"

Suzy didn't answer. Dane reached out and took her hand as they crossed the street. "Hey, it wasn't so bad."

"I have a feeling," Suzy said, "that our business merger is being hijacked by the kindest people on earth."

"Nah," he said, "we're still in control. Let's get a ring and then—"

"I vote we don't," she said. "It's not cost-effective, considering the plan."

"On the contrary. The ladies are watching us from the courthouse window, and we don't want anyone to say that we're not the town's happiest couple, do we?"

"And in a year, when they think we're the town's most quickly divorced couple?"

Dane knew Suzy was thinking about her daughters' future in Union Junction. He couldn't blame her. "Let's go in and look. Then they'll be satisfied."

"All right."

She sounded as if the spirit of adventure had left her. Dane opened the door and they went inside the jeweler's.

It was a replay of the courthouse incident, with the elderly Mr. Tompkins not only inviting himself to the wedding, but selecting their bands—a very affordable set of white gold rings. Suzy's even had a trail of diamonds along the top that made it sparkle. He wouldn't accept payment—said he'd bill them—and sent them on their way with a lot of hearty good wishes and the request that they say hello to old Josiah for him.

Dane helped Suzy into his truck. "None of this will matter in a few months."

She looked at him from the seat of his truck. He'd hesitated, not closing the door just yet, stealing one last lingering look at her solemn face. She was just so cute, all worried about money, that he almost felt bad that he'd talked her into this plan. But then he remembered how much she wanted the Morgan name for her children and felt better about sharing it with her.

"Don't worry, Suzy," he said softly, catching her hands in his. And then, not caring that plenty of people were watching them with avid and delighted interest, he kissed his new fiancée on the hand, then her lips, just like he'd been wanting to for days.

Chapter Thirteen

Suzy's breath caught as Dane kissed her. He took his time with her lips, turning all the anxiety she'd been feeling into a bone-melting promise she welcomed.

The first time he'd kissed her, she'd been annoyed and a little scared.

But now his lips were soft, gentle, searching. Suzy felt herself closing her eyes, leaning forward to receive more of Dane's kiss. Her blood seemed to buzz; her hands slid up his arms.

Then she remembered where she was—on the main street of Union Junction with an audience—and she pulled herself away. His eyes sparkled at her, his lips turned up in a teasing quirk.

"If you like being a fiancée this much, imagine how much fun being married will be," he said, and Suzy groaned.

"Could we get home?" she asked. "I'm sure my girls are wondering where I am."

"Not with their aunties Cricket and Priscilla bribing

them with sweets and hugs. I'm sure they're in the best of hands, but, yes, we'll hit the road." He pulled away from the curb, waving to each friendly person watching them drive by. "It surprises me that so many people have such warm regard for Pop."

"Josiah's done a lot for many of us." Suzy stared down at her ring, amazed that she wore such a beautiful gift on her finger. She felt guilty accepting it, but Dane had insisted, said it was for the girls, too, and how could she refuse such sentiment? He seemed to mention the girls and their future often, and his concern for them warmed her. Maybe Dane *was* more like his father than she'd thought.

"Funny what money can do," Dane said, "including turning people's opinions around."

"Josiah never said why you all didn't like each other," Suzy commented carefully.

He shook his head. "He was hard on us. Wanted us to be men. Thought the world beat people down who didn't know how to take care of themselves. And still, we could have stood that, because it was us four boys against him, so we stayed bonded together. But one night—"

He hesitated. Suzy looked at him. "One night?"

"One night we sneaked out. We wanted to see Jack ride in the rodeo. Pop was harder on Jack than the rest of us because he was the oldest. I think Pop wanted Jack to be tough enough to raise us if anything happened to him. This was a long time ago, before Union Junction had grown so much. Basically, we were country kids, far out from the town. Pop didn't have many friends.

Our mother had left when we were young because she was tired of Pop's traveling. She went back home to France. I think it was hard being foreign here, and alone in the country with no other women for companionship." He shrugged. "I don't really know what made her leave. I've always assumed he treated her as roughly as he treated us with his tough love."

"So she left?"

"Yeah. So Jack was supposed to be responsible for us. But he was a kid, too, and he loved the one thing Pop hated, which was rodeo. In Pop's eyes, rodeo was the sin of loafing, ne'er-do-well ill-bred types. This was in the days before sponsorships and a living could be made at it."

Suzy remembered her well-heeled parents attending cocktail parties and dinner balls for charities. She'd been trotted out in various gowns and bows when she was a child to greet the guests before being taken back upstairs by the nanny. Like a doll, she'd enjoyed putting on her shoes and having her hair done high and being introduced as the only daughter of the wealthy Winterstones. Of course, she'd been a debutante, and an eastern Ivy League education would have followed a summer abroad at Oxford.

But she'd chosen nursing school at the local community college, feeling more comfortable in her own element. She'd met the man she'd fallen in love with, her first love…only to have her eyes cruelly opened to discover that the love was one-sided. Her parents had been devastated and humiliated by her pregnancy. An ex-cop or a rodeo cowboy would never have been her parents' choice for her. "So Jack was independent," she murmured.

"Which drove Pop nuts because he saw Jack throwing away his life on something that paid nothing. But we loved watching him ride. We didn't have the courage to disobey Pop and do it ourselves, but we sure did like watching Jack." He took a deep breath. "But one night we sneaked out to watch him, and there was an accident…we got hit by a driver who shouldn't have been on the road. Pop never forgave Jack for being a bad example. He was so mad at him. It was fury I never saw even in my years in the military or in the Rangers."

"And then what?" Suzy asked, not wanting to cause him more pain but having to know what had driven Josiah and his boys apart.

"We lied to cover for Jack. Said it was each other's idea to go." He shook his head. "We were young, confused, scared for Jack, who was in the hospital after a bad ride. In the end, we all got in so much trouble, we just ran away. I know that sounds cowardly, but Pop had always been pretty hard to live with. We were afraid. That's all there is to it. And we made bad choices."

Suzy hesitated. She couldn't offer any words of consolation or advice because she knew too well what it felt like to earn a parent's scorn. Their judgment destroyed the trust a child felt with their parent, whom they wanted to be able to count on. "I'm sorry," she finally said.

"Don't be," Dane said, his voice hard, "it's all in the past."

And yet it's not, Suzy thought. *It's right here in this truck with us, and it's the reason we're saying I do.*

DANE TOOK A LONG TIME THINKING about whether or not he would call Pop. The conversation would be awkward; there was a lot unsaid between them.

Yet the townspeople had made him think about his father's feelings, and how much Pop liked Suzy. And so in the end, he decided to call and tell his father they were getting married, for Suzy's sake. He could tell it bothered her that her parents had disowned her, which was probably why she'd appreciated Josiah looking after her and Sandra and Nicole.

And so, if Dane was falling in with his father's plans—at least on the surface—then it would be best for everyone if he let Josiah know he had won. Dane drank a beer, wandered around the barns for a while, and finally forced himself to pull out the phone in his bedroom and place the call.

"Hello?" Josiah barked.

Dane hesitated. Josiah was no smaller a personality when he was a few countries away; Dane could feel himself snapping to attention as soon as he heard his father's voice. "Pop, it's Dane."

"Dane? To what do I owe the honor of this phone call?" Josiah demanded.

So much for pleasantries. "Pop, just wanted to let you know that…" He stopped, fought with his conscience, knowing that Pop would feel vindicated just like with

Gabriel…and yet, it wasn't about Pop. This call, and the wedding, was about Suzy. "I'm getting married, Pop."

"To whom, may I ask?" His father's voice was only mildly curious.

"Suzy Winterstone," Dane said.

Josiah chuckled. "Best of luck to you," he said.

That was it? Dane frowned. "Thank you."

"Thank you for calling," Josiah said courteously.

The line went dead. Dane stared at the phone for a moment, somewhat stunned. That was it? He'd agonized over calling his father, hadn't spoken fifty words to him in ten years, and that was all Josiah had to say?

The man was, like everyone had once said, a jackass.

Only he wasn't really called that much anymore. Dane reflected on that, and why it was so difficult to thaw the relationship between Josiah and his boys. "That was anticlimactic," he said to himself.

He went to find Suzy. She was in the kitchen with Priscilla, Cricket and the twins. They were drawing frosting decorations on a piece of paper, presumably planning for cakes.

"Swirls or bows?" Cricket asked Dane.

"Uh—"

The ladies all laughed at his expression.

"That means, don't bother me with the details," Priscilla said. "You look tired, Dane."

Suzy glanced at him, her gaze questioning. "I called Pop," he told her.

"And?"

He shrugged, reached into the fridge for a beer. "He said congratulations, and that I couldn't have picked a finer woman."

"See?" Cricket said. "Josiah's softening up in his old age."

Suzy's eyes widened. She went back to examining patterns on the paper, so Dane slid into a seat and pulled the twins up into his lap. "You girls need a coloring table," he told them. "Someplace where you can sit and color, with tiny seats and a tiny table that's made just for pint-sized arts and crafts. I'm going to build you one."

Suzy glanced up. "They'd love that! Their own little workstation." She beamed at him, and he felt himself puffing up with pride. "I didn't know you could build things, Dane."

For the first time since meeting Suzy and her girls, Dane felt valuable. He didn't know why he hadn't felt this before, because Suzy seemed to admire him, when she wasn't being shy. But there'd been hero worship in her tone just then, and he'd liked it—this was the first time in his life anyone had ever been amazed by something he could do.

He could feel himself wanting to brag a little, get some more attention from her, and had to fight the urge. "It's not as hard to build a table as it is to bake wedding cakes, I bet."

Priscilla smiled at his efforts to praise them in return. "Suzy, this man is a prince."

Suzy looked at Dane, slowly lowering her eyes. She

hadn't been so shy when he'd kissed her in Union Junction. In fact, she'd seemed quite eager, unless he was misreading her signals. She peeked up at him again, a soft smile on her face, and that's when Dane knew he wasn't quite the businessman his father was.

His heart was definitely getting involved.

SUZY HAD PUT THE GIRLS TO BED, and Cricket and Priscilla were off in their rooms when she heard a knock on her door. She opened it to find Dane standing outside. "Hi."

"Hi." He cleared his throat. "Are the girls asleep?"

She nodded. "They drifted off without protest."

He smiled. "When I called Pop, he didn't seem as surprised as I thought he'd be."

Suzy moved into the room to fold some of Sandra's and Nicole's tiny clothes. "It's hard to surprise your father. He's made a living not letting people catch him off guard."

"But you and my father weren't in cahoots?"

She looked at him, not exactly shocked that he'd ask but not pleased at the implications of what he'd said, either. "I would do a lot of things for my children's futures, but drag a man to the altar isn't one of them, obviously, or I'd be married now."

"Sorry," he said, looking apologetic. "I didn't really think you would, but I just expected more of a reaction from Pop."

"You don't show a lot of emotion yourself," Suzy pointed out. "Maybe it runs in the family."

"I never gave it much thought."

"Jack strikes me as the most emotional of all of you," Suzy said. "He gets his feelings hurt easily."

"Tell me about it." He shook his head. "Well, just thought I'd tell you I spoke with Pop. He didn't seem particularly happy. He didn't seem much of anything. So if you're doing this for the old man's sake, he may not care one way or the other. I guess what I'm trying to say is, don't marry me out of a sense of obligation to Pop."

She considered his suggestion. "If you're not planning to accept your money, and your father's not thrilled you're here, why are you still marrying me? Perhaps you're the one who's acting out of obligation."

He stared at her. With a sinking heart, she realized he didn't have any reason to marry her; he was, in fact, acting out of duty and responsibility—to her. Probably more specifically, to her daughters, because Josiah had wanted him to look after Suzy and her girls. Whether Dane realized it or not, he was seeking his father's approval.

"I see," Suzy said softly. "You thought your father would be proud of you. When you called him and told him the good news, you thought you were doing what would make him happy. Being a good son. Giving him grandchildren, and a reason to believe you were home to stay."

"I don't think that was what my motives were," Dane said.

"Every man wants to know his father loves him and thinks well of him."

"It matters more than I thought it would," Dane admitted, "but I'm not backing out now."

"Obligation?" Suzy asked.

"I don't feel sorry for you," Dane murmured. "You're too independent. But you and your girls represent something good in my life, and I don't feel like giving it up now. Not this soon."

She held her breath for a moment. Her ex had never said anything like that to her. Coming from Dane, the words sounded more romantic than obliged. She wanted to believe him. It was so hard, given what she knew about men, and though she tried to judge Dane on his own merits, what she knew about him was that he liked his freedom. "So now what?"

"I'm sticking it out here, without taking Pop's money, if for no other reason than to prove to him that I'm choosing how to live my life of my own free will. I'll always know that I did my part to put away the past."

She nodded slowly, understanding.

"Now the decision is up to you," he said, his tone steady. "We can live here, or we can live at your house, your choice. But I'd like to change the business proposition. Instead of getting married because Pop's pulling the strings, I'd like the next three hundred sixty-two days of marriage to answer a different question."

"What would that be?" she asked, her heart beginning to beat faster. Dane's gaze on her was so purposeful that Suzy knew that the phone call to his father had changed Dane.

"If we still want to stay married after a year," he said, drawing her to him for a long, sweet kiss, "I hope you'll let me adopt your girls."

Chapter Fourteen

"He's romancing you," Cricket said when Suzy told her about Dane's new proposal. "Something's changed him."

They looked out the window while Dane worked down by the barn. Chips of wood flew, and smoke and sawdust swirled around the electric saw. Suzy could almost smell the fresh-cut wood as he worked on the children's table he'd promised Sandra and Nicole.

Priscilla nodded. "It's an astonishing transformation. Maybe he's falling in love with you."

Suzy didn't know what to think. "Or maybe he's falling in love with being a father."

Cricket smiled. "People do change. Their priorities change. Maybe Dane wants different things out of life than he thought he did before."

"I don't know," Suzy said. "Maybe this is just family responsibility he's shouldering without realizing it." She watched Dane, his muscles bunched under his T-shirt as he worked. He wore plastic protective glasses, and his cowboy hat. The two didn't necessarily go together, but Suzy still thought he made an attractive sight.

"I suppose Josiah could have made the water so muddy Dane doesn't really know why he wants to marry you," Cricket said. "Not to be mean or anything, but it does seem like what Josiah can't give emotionally, he gives monetarily. Or at least people certainly seem to respect his generous donations to the town. I've had five phone calls this morning from ladies in Union Junction wanting to know what they can do to help with the wedding."

Suzy gasped. "We're not inviting the whole town!"

"I don't know," Priscilla said. "A lot of people are anxious to do something for Josiah."

She was in a dilemma. Only she knew the truth about the elder Mr. Morgan—his health was seriously failing. This wedding could be one way to bring him home, to be around his family while he still had some time.

"Did Dane actually invite him to the wedding?" Priscilla asked.

"I don't know," Suzy said. "I don't think so, because he didn't mention it."

"Well, his friends in Union Junction certainly seem to think he's coming back."

Suzy straightened. "That's why he wasn't surprised about the wedding. Someone had already called him."

Priscilla nodded. "I would believe that. The Union Junction grapevine runs at the speed of light. And apparently reaches all the way to France."

Cricket smiled. "What are you going to do about all the want-to-be-guests?"

"We're getting married in three nights, on Saturday," Suzy said. "We don't really know who Josiah's friends are, and we don't want to accidentally leave anyone out. Besides, we think it's best handled as a private matter, since it's a short-term agreement we're undertaking."

Cricket shook her head. "As a deacon, I have to warn against underestimating the seriousness of marital vows. They can be potentially binding, since that's the intent."

Priscilla's cell phone rang. Answering it, she listened intently, then said, "That would be lovely. I'll mention it to Dane and Suzy, but we certainly appreciate the help." She hung up and looked at Suzy. "Your wedding's been hijacked by your father-in-law-to-be."

Suzy just stared at her, suspecting the worst.

"Josiah has already put the word out that there's a huge wedding at the Morgan ranch on Saturday night. There'll be enough barbecue and wedding cake for everyone who wants to attend. So say the ladies at the courthouse. Oh, and by the way, it's supposed to be Josiah's wedding present to you and Dane, but Celie was bursting to tell me. I wasn't supposed to ruin the surprise, but, being your friend, figured I'd better." Priscilla smiled at her. "Good thing they didn't call Cricket, who might have felt honored to keep a secret."

"Oh, no," Suzy murmured. "This is not good."

"And you said you trusted Josiah," Cricket said with a laugh. "Better pick another Morgan to trust."

"I guess I'll go tell Dane," Suzy said. "Maybe he'll decide to back out." She couldn't help thinking of her ex, who couldn't handle marriage and responsibility. Dane was a man made of stronger stuff, wasn't he?

Of course, he'd once told her his fondest wish was to open a parasailing business in Mexico. Shivering in the January chill, she walked to the barn. She waited until Dane glanced up and saw her before approaching him. He turned off the saw and pushed his goggles up.

"Hey. I've just about got all the wood cut," he said proudly.

"It looks great. The girls will love having their own big-girls table."

He nodded. "Just right for little hands and legs."

"Your father has planned a surprise wedding for us," Suzy blurted. "The whole town is invited to the ranch to have barbecue and wedding cake."

Dane looked at her, his mouth quirking into a wry smile. "I should be mad."

"Yes. We both should."

"He's an interfering old donkey."

She nodded. "He does seem anxious to do things his way."

Dane laid the saw down. "Does that mean Pop's coming home for the wedding?"

"I don't know. It would be nice if he could."

He wiped off his hands on a bandana. "I apologize for my father. He's always done things his way."

"I think he's trying to do something special for us," Suzy said, but Dane shook his head.

"Actually, he's stepped over the line. I can call him back—"

Suzy sighed. "It wouldn't do any good. If we told him we didn't want a big wedding, people's feelings would be hurt. Everybody in Union Junction loves your father and is looking forward to a big party."

"I think you're right."

"Well, we have your father who cares too much, and mine who cares not at all," Suzy said, trying to sound bright yet not feeling that way. "It balances out."

Dane watched her silently.

She took a deep breath. "About adopting my girls," she said, "thank you for offering. I don't know what made you do that."

"I wouldn't normally take that as a compliment, but it sounds like you're trying to give me one."

"I am." She nodded. "I didn't know what to say to you about adopting the girls—you really touched me. And I still don't know if that would be the best decision for us, honestly." She looked into his eyes, hoping he would understand. "But it's the nicest thing anyone has ever tried to do for my girls since your father's gift of a college education. Only this is even more special, to me."

He nodded. "The offer's there. It's not going anywhere."

Suzy felt tears jump into her eyes. "Thank you."

He opened his hands as if to say "no problem."

"I think," Suzy said, willing her throat to relax from the emotions sweeping her, "I think we go along with your father's wedding plans without complaint. Try to enjoy the celebration."

"Just fall in with the old man? He may never stop running things."

"It's only a wedding," Suzy said quietly, "it's not the marriage he's interfering with."

"True." Dane nodded. "Guess we'll just roll with it, then."

Relieved, Suzy said, "I'll see you later."

Nodding, he replaced his goggles and went back to sawing wood. Suzy watched him for another moment, wondering if Dane knew how much his father loved him—and if Dane would care.

DANE'S CONSCIENCE BUGGED HIM. It had been pestering him for a while. He thought he understood his father. He fully comprehended why Pop was so anxious about Suzy. The woman had a vulnerable side she tried to mask but couldn't completely conceal—it made a man want to protect her. He doubted she'd appreciate the sentiment. Having made up her mind that she was a single mother and going to be a darn good one, Suzy wanted no pity or favors from anyone.

Her strength made him admire her. Her vulnerability made him want to take care of her and the girls. Her sadness over her parents' and boyfriend's desertion of her when she needed them most broke his heart.

Dane showered and then got in his truck to drive to Fort Wylie. There was a time in every man's life when he had to look to the past. His father was well-renowned as a stubborn man—though he seemed to be rectifying his reputation—and some of that stubbornness surely had etched itself into Dane. Despite the suddenly elaborate wedding plans, the wonderful cakes, the loads of food, Dane didn't feel that the wedding was really official.

It came down to one simple thing: He had not yet asked Suzy's father for her hand in marriage. And because he was a stubborn man, Dane had begun to realize that he had to have this one thing done his way. He was a conservative, traditional man by nature. It didn't sit right with him that he hadn't paid the respect to Suzy's father that the occasion deserved.

If the man booted him off his porch, it would be Mr. Winterstone's right, but at least he'd know that he'd honored the special moment a father only knew once in his life.

If it were him—and Sandra and Nicole were his daughters—he'd want some young pup to have the fortitude to show respect to him and the occasion, no matter what the circumstances were.

Dane intended to do that. After all, he was the son of a hardheaded man—and Suzy should probably know what she was getting herself into now while she still had time to back out.

He finally arrived at the Winterstones' mansion. A wrought-iron gate across the driveway kept unwanted guests away. He wasn't certain whether or not he would be welcomed, so he buzzed the intercom and waited.

"Yes?" a voice inquired through the intercom.

"I'm here to see Mr. and Mrs. Winterstone," Dane said.

"Dr. Winterstone," the voice corrected.

"I beg your pardon. Dr. Winterstone," Dane said. "My name is Dane Morgan. I'm here on behalf of Suzy Winterstone."

"I will ask Dr. and Mrs. Winterstone if they are receiving," the voice said.

"You do that," Dane muttered to himself, enjoying the chilly air circulating inside the truck. He was sweating, he realized—actually perspiring, with a case of nerves only a real bridegroom might suffer. He hadn't anticipated the size of the mansion, the heavy, protective fence, the cold-voiced housekeeper—no wonder Suzy got tense just thinking about her parents. He almost felt as if he were visiting a castle, a knight riding in to get his head lopped off by an easily irked ruler.

A vision of palm trees waving in Mexico jumped into his head. Dane gripped white-knuckled fingers around the steering wheel, telling himself he wasn't bolting. If these people didn't want to meet their prospective son-in-law, then it sure wasn't anything that would keep him up at night.

Yeah, it would. For Suzy's sake, he wanted harmony between him and her folks. He knew too well what a heavy load hard feelings could be—and the fact was, if her parents were holding her hostage with their disapproval of her having children out of wedlock, then they were only hurting themselves. Sandra and Nicole were awesome kids, destined to be ladies in Suzy's mold.

The gate slowly slid back. Dane blinked in disbelief. *Here we go.* Taking a deep breath, he drove up the circular driveway, stopping in front of marble steps.

A uniformed man appeared at his open window. "Good evening, sir."

Dane nodded. "Good evening."

"I'll park your car for you, sir."

"I'm parked. It's good here." Dane turned off the truck, got out and patted the man on the back. "No need to stand on ceremony for me. No one can drive this truck but me. She's got two hundred thousand miles on her and has a lot of quirks."

"Yes, sir." The man pointed to the steps. "The housekeeper will take you to the Winterstones."

"Good man, good man." Dane jogged up the steps to the double front door. "Howdy," he said to the housekeeper. "You must have been the sexy voice on the intercom."

The elderly woman looked at him haughtily, her gaze taking in his flannel shirt, jeans, boots and well-worn hat. "Your name, sir?"

"Dane Morgan."

"This way, please."

He followed her, struck by how giant, how imposing this house was. And he'd thought Pop's ranch was overwhelming! The home where Suzy had grown up was palatial, aristocratic.

Suddenly he realized why Suzy wasn't just jumping for joy to marry him and had never cared about the money. She'd always had money. She could have continued living this lifestyle had she not fallen in love with the wrong man. No wonder she was willing to marry Dane without love. She'd already had wealth and it had turned on her. She liked her independence. Suzy could count on herself and that was all she planned to rely on.

The only reason she'd agreed to marry him was because he'd offered her his last name for her girls.

It was the only thing he had to give her.

He was ushered into a formal sitting area with a fireplace and pristine white sofas. Two small, middle-aged people stood as he entered the room. Behind him, the housekeeper closed the door.

"Hello, Dr. Winterstone and Mrs. Winterstone," he said. "My name is Dane Morgan." They didn't draw near him so he knew they had no intention of shaking his hand.

"We know your name," Dr. Winterstone said. "You apparently have come on an errand from Suzy."

"Not an errand," Dane said, deciding he had nothing to lose at this point by being a bit frosty himself. He was trying to throw these people a lifeline, if they would only realize it. He thought about Sandra and Nicole and their chance to know their grandparents, and told himself to play nice. He was doing this just as much for the girls as for Suzy—he didn't want to fail them. Surely somewhere in these stiff people resided hearts that beat warm blood. "I've come to ask you for Suzy's hand in marriage."

"Well," Mrs. Winterstone said, "if that's all you came for, you needn't have bothered. Suzy has been on her own for some time. I'm sure she's capable of accepting you herself without our guidance, of which she thinks very little, we can assure you."

There was a lot of hurt and anger in Mrs. Winterstone's voice. Dane shifted, since he hadn't been invited to take a seat, deciding that he and his future in-laws would never be close so he might as well press forward with the greater goal in mind. "Your daughter doesn't know I'm here. I came out of respect to you, because no matter the circumstances of the past between you and Suzy, it's important to me to look to the future."

"All right, Mr. Morgan," Dr. Winterstone said. "Since you claim to be trying to observe traditional niceties, tell me what you do for a living and how you propose to care for Suzy and her child."

"Children," Dane said. "Sandra and Nicole." He noticed a flicker of surprise in Mrs. Winterstone's gaze as she glanced at her husband. "She had twins. They're adorable, I must say. Busy as beavers, and guaranteed to bring a smile to your face."

"You were telling us what you do for a living, Mr. Morgan," Suzy's father said.

"I'm retired from the Texas Rangers."

"Baseball player?" her father asked, his bushy white eyebrows rising on his broad forehead.

"Law enforcement," Dane clarified.

"I see. You've retired young on a public servant's salary," the doctor said. "Did you save enough money to take care of a family of four? Make wise investments, perhaps? Have a plan for the future?"

"Well," Dane said with a grin, "I'd have to say no, no and no."

"So then we might assume that you're marrying Suzy because of her family connections and our wealth," Dr. Winterstone said. Mrs. Winterstone sank into a white sofa, staring up at Dane with some horror.

"Wealth?" Dane repeated. "She actually never mentioned anything about money."

"You don't expect us to believe that," Dr. Winterstone scoffed.

"With God as my witness, I had no idea. To be honest, it's a bit conspicuous, don't you think?" Dane asked conversationally. "How does someone make this much money?"

"It's inherited wealth, something of which you would have no knowledge," Dr. Winterstone said. "We keep our wealth by not making rash decisions."

"Oh, I'd disagree with that," Dane said. "You've got two darling granddaughters that are worth more than every marble bust in this room."

"Having never had two dimes to rub together," Dr. Winterstone said, "perhaps you are not in a position to judge what is valuable in life, although I do appreciate the sentiment about Suzy's children."

He and Dane stared at each other.

"Just as a final curiosity," the gentleman said, "can I ask you where you're from?"

"The Morgan ranch," Dane said proudly, for the first time in his life.

"Ah, farmers," Dr. Winterstone mused. "Is that your plan now? To try your hand at the boom and bust of Mother Nature and the commodity cycle?"

"Actually, I'd planned to move to Mexico and open a parasailing business," Dane said cheerfully, "but that was until I met your daughter. Now I'm thinking I may sell some pecans, raise some horses…I haven't really figured it all out. Yet." He grinned at Suzy's parents. "But you can be sure I will."

"Thank you for the promise of that," Doctor Winterstone said. "But I'm certain you'll understand that, if you were asking me for my daughter's hand and this wasn't a rhetorical exercise, I'd have to tell you you'd need to return when you'd figured out a little bit more about the basics of life, such as food and shelter."

"It's a shame," Dane said, "you're going to miss out on a real wingding of a wedding. We're having barbecue and all the cake you can eat, made by Suzy's friends."

Mrs. Winterstone fanned herself with a *Town and Country* magazine. "Barbecue," she said faintly.

"Sure. It's a wedding gift from my dad." Dane couldn't help chuckling. "I won't keep you two any longer. We're getting married this weekend, so if you feel like taking a drive into the far country, you'll find us exchanging rings at the Morgan ranch outside of Union Junction proper. Ask anybody and they can tell you how to get there. Be sure you ask early because everybody in town is invited, so the town will probably close up early."

"Why would the whole town want to come to your wedding?" Mrs. Winterstone asked. "It hardly sounds like the social event of the season."

"Well, people like Suzy, for one thing," Dane said. "And my pop is known around town as a real—" he started to say *jackass* and then realized the man he was standing across from made Pop look like an angel "—a real generous man," he finished, telling the truth and proud of it. "You'd probably like him, Dr. Winterstone. Think you two would have a lot in common. I'm not sure he's going to be there," Dane said, "but he happens to think your daughter and granddaughters hung the moon." He turned to walk himself to the door.

"Where is your father, may I ask, if not in his own home?" Dr. Winterstone asked. "I presume the Morgan ranch is his, and you're living with your father?"

"Pop lives in France," Dane said simply. "He likes the peace and quiet." He put his hat back on and walked himself to the door, not waiting for the housekeeper to open it for him. "Thanks," he said, "but where I'm from, we know how to do things for ourselves."

Once outside, he saw the uniformed attendant hurrying to open his truck door. Dane walked across the circle driveway. "Don't bother," he said. "I can take it from here."

The man wasn't sure what to think about Dane. Dane grinned at him, slapped him on the back and said, "Take good care of them," as he got into his truck and drove away.

Chapter Fifteen

Two hours later, Dane pulled into the Morgan ranch, feeling the familiarity of the surroundings wrap around him like a comfortable blanket. The Winterstones might like their castle, but give him fresh air and wide-open spaces any day. The more time he spent at the ranch, the more he felt himself falling in love with the country, which held a different kind of freedom than he would probably find in Mexico.

Now he knew he'd simply been running away from the things he needed to face. Like Dr. Winterstone had said, he was a man with no prospects. The good doctor might have decided his daughter wasn't worth his time, but he had pointed out that Suzy deserved respect and a man who could take good care of her as a provider.

Dane resolved to do just that. He headed to find his fiancée, discovering her making play-dough art with her toddlers, who were sitting at the little table he'd made for them. They looked so cute—like their mother in adorable miniature. Cricket and Priscilla weren't there—probably off cooking up wedding plans—so he bent down and kissed Suzy on the lips the way he meant to kiss her every night for the year that they planned to be married. He wasn't wasting any time. Life was short and needed to be enjoyed to the fullest—or he might end up in a white room with marble statues of dead people wearing persnickety frowns.

Suzy stared at him in shock when he finally pulled away from her. "Was there a reason for that?"

"None at all," he said. "Just be prepared for me to claim my kiss every single night of the year you've promised to be married to me. I am not a man who plans to live with regret any longer."

"Does that mean you've invited your father to the wedding?" Suzy asked.

"No, it means I asked your father for your hand in marriage, like a proper bridegroom should."

Suzy's mouth fell open. Then a frown gathered on her forehead. "I wish you had not."

"I should have told you," he said, looking down into her eyes, "but I knew you'd try to talk me out of it. There are certain things a man just has to do."

She looked away. "I should say thank you, but I'm angry that you went without telling me."

"It will be the only time I ever keep something from you," Dane said, kneeling beside her. "You have my word on that."

"Thank you." She looked at him. "I won't interfere with your father anymore, either."

"Not possible." He shook his head. "Pop loves to be interfered with. All the drama and intrigue keep his heart beating."

"I hope my parents treated you somewhat kindly," she said, her posture stiff.

He could tell her feelings were badly bruised by her parents' attitude. Glancing over at Sandra and Nicole and their play-dough art, it wasn't too hard to see why Suzy would feel pained by her folks' abandonment. "Growing up with Pop was good training for dealing with people like your parents," he said simply. And then it occurred to him that Pop, rough in his ways as he was, had been trying to raise his sons with a shield of armor to protect them from the occasional unkindnesses of life. "Actually, your folks made Pop seem generous in the emotions department."

She hesitated. "I'm past needing their approval."

She wasn't and he knew it. "I'm sure they'll thaw in time. In the meantime, we know why we're getting married. Nothing's changed."

Her expression went blank. She put away the children's crafts and washed their hands, quietly taking the girls upstairs without another word to Dane.

SUZY COULDN'T EXPLAIN her sadness to Dane. It was humiliating that her parents could act so rudely. Dane hadn't told her all the details, but she knew the icy Winterstone treatment of outsiders to their social circle. She knew exactly to what he'd been subjected.

He'd treated her so nicely when he'd returned, trying to protect her pride. She hated that. She didn't want to be pitied for her parents' handling of her—and didn't want Dane to think she would ever turn into someone as cold and emotionless as either of them.

The whole issue of coldness bothered her. Remote, was what her boyfriend had said, in bed and out of it. That had hurt. He'd compared her emotional aloofness to her parents'. Maybe she had been aloof. Mostly she was shy. As an only child of a family who had staff to do everything for them, she hadn't known a lot of easy affection. For all their faults the Morgans boasted of—usually proudly—they were an emotional group of men.

None of them would admit that about themselves. They thought they were so strong and practical in their approach to life. She'd grown up practically, and the Morgans were definitely cut from different cloth. They were hot-blooded, stubborn, determined. Impatient. And proud of holding grudges.

In her world, people who didn't fit were simply cut out, like undesirable fabric on a gown. She gently dressed her girls in their nightgowns, smiling at their pleasure in their frilly, long, pink nighties. Slowly she brushed their soft, silky hair, and then helped them brush their very small teeth. This was her favorite part of the evening, the quiet time that she shared only with her girls. Putting away the day's toys, slipping into clean sheets, reading a story with the girls raptly watching her read every word on every page—and they knew if she skipped anything.

"Hey." She heard a knock on the door and Dane's voice, so she poked her head out of the bathroom.

"Yes?"

"Do you have a minute?"

"I'm getting the girls ready for bed—"

Sandra and Nicole ran from the bathroom to throw their arms around Dane's legs, destroying the serenity of the routine. "Sorry about that," he said, "I didn't realize it was so late."

"It's all right. Sandra, Nicole, hop up into your beds, please."

The girls did as she asked but pulled Dane along with them, handing him their storybook. He looked up at Suzy, his eyes questioning. "I'm being auditioned for a speaking role," he said, "do you mind?"

She did, a little selfishly, since these were her treasured moments with her children, and she didn't want Dane moving further into her heart. Though she hadn't said it, she was secretly pleased he'd gone to show her father respect. It said that he intended to honor their marriage with the same importance he might attach to marrying a woman with whom he was in love. He treated Sandra and Nicole as if they were very precious to him—maybe even part of his own family.

She loved that about him.

She did not want to fall in love with him, though. She couldn't endure another heartbreak. Nor did she want her girls to suffer heartbreak. They were young, they'd hardly know when Dane left. But Suzy would remember for them.

She steeled her nerves. "Please go right ahead. I'll use the time to write down the flowers I want to carry in my bouquet. Cricket insists she can make the bouquet herself, so she wants a list."

He grinned. "Resourceful."

She nodded. "Wait until you see the dress they chose."

His grin widened. "Really?"

"It's very simple, very lovely. What I would have always wanted," she said.

"How did they do that?"

He seemed genuinely interested—unlike most men would be about women's clothing—so she said, "Priscilla said she had a friend in Tulips, Texas, who designed gowns. She described what I wanted, and it turned out her friend, Liberty, had the exact dress in stock."

Dane was still grinning. "I can't wait for the wedding night."

She froze, and he did, too.

Neither of them said a word. Their gazes met for a long, painful moment, before Sandra jostled his arm and pointed to the page where he should begin reading.

The moment broken, Suzy went to find a notepad to make a list, noticing the rapidness of her pulse and the sudden nervousness she felt about her wedding two nights from now.

In three nights, she would be sharing a bed with Dane

Morgan. It was all she could do to make herself breathe deeply, calmly. But the strange thing was, she wasn't sure if she was excited or panicked—or both.

IT WASN'T EASY BEING A MAN. Dane knew that women thought guys just operated on sex and other basic behaviors that resulted in their own pleasure—like sleeping and eating—but what Suzy didn't know is that she was driving him nuts. He couldn't stop thinking about her, and that alone was enough to make him sleepless and edgy.

At some point, she'd gotten to him, just like Pete had said.

He supposed he'd fallen first for her children—a strange thought for a hardened bachelor. But meeting Suzy's parents had awakened in him a realization that he and Suzy were kindred spirits. They belonged together.

Maybe it was just her father's anger and disapproval that made him want to be her armor against the storms, protecting her from her parents' coldness. But that didn't explain the hunger for her that assailed him at every opportunity. He found himself wanting to touch her, to be with her, to sneak a kiss from her whenever he could.

After the wedding, he planned to kiss her often, until she matched his need for her.

He called Gabriel to ask him to be his best man. Gabriel suggested Mason Jefferson to be an usher and offered to call him. After he hung up, Dane wondered what else he should do. What else fell under the groom's responsibilities?

"Hey!" Dane heard whispered urgently at his bedroom door. "Dane!"

Sounded like Pete. If he kept on like that, he might wake the little girls. Dane opened the door, shocked to find Jack outside.

"Jack! What the hell?" Dane said, relieved and yet somewhat freaked out to see his long-lost brother.

Jack slipped inside the room. "You look good."

Dane closed the door. "Thanks. You look tired."

Jack nodded.

"How'd you know this is my room?"

"Only light on upstairs that I could see from the ground floor. The ladies are in the kitchen poring over flower book arrangements."

His brother was leaner, longer, whip-thin. Dane could hardly believe it was Jack in the flesh and not some road-worn ghost. "Have a seat," he said, pointing to his desk chair.

"Can't. Have to hit the road. Heard through the grapevine that you're getting hitched," Jack said.

"Grapevine?"

"Pete left a note for me at the rodeo, along with an artifact he found from Pop." Jack pulled it out. "The old man is determined to make my life miserable."

"Well, not just yours. What did the letter say? Wait, how the hell does Pete know I'm getting married?"

Jack shrugged. "He said it was only a matter of time before you fell under the bus."

"The bus?"

"Pop and his planning. The runaway bus."

"Oh, jeez." Dane rubbed his chin. "So, anyway. Why are you here? There has to be a darn good reason."

Jack nodded. "This letter from Pop is bad luck for me. I can't ride with this hanging over my head."

Dane blinked. "Superstitious?"

"Oh, yeah. They say the sins of the father are visited on the sons, you know."

"Something like that."

Jack leaned forward. "The letter says,

Jack,

I tried to be a good father. I tried to save you from yourself. In the end, I realized that you are too different from me. But I was always proud of my firstborn son."

He looked up at Dane. "Bad karma."

Dane hesitated. "I didn't know Pop could express emotion. Doesn't that seem positive?"

Jack shook his head. "Dane, I can't pick up where we left off over ten years ago. I can't just forgive the old man. That may sound harsh, but he was a terrible father. Riding bulls is the only time I'm free from him."

Dane didn't figure he was ever free from the old man, not since he'd returned to the ranch. "I don't think he wants us free. Isn't that the purpose of getting us all out here?"

"Precisely. Pete's note said that this letter was

found in a kitchen drawer. I think Pop meant for me to have it after—"

Dane frowned. "After?"

Jack sighed. "This is a goodbye letter."

Chapter Sixteen

Unease swept Dane. He stared at Jack, who seemed completely convinced of his hypothesis. "I saw Pop last June. He was as ornery as ever, which I would take as a sign he's not on his way to St. Peter's gates."

"Okay," Jack said, "but I hear he's been putting the pressure on for grandkids."

Dane shrugged. "I don't know that it's pressure exactly—"

"Are you getting married because of Pop?" Jack asked, crossing his arms.

Dane considered Jack's question. "Maybe in the beginning I was—"

A frown crossed Jack's face. "Maybe in the beginning you were? What does that mean?"

"A million dollars is a lot of money. My plan was that I'd marry Suzy, like I figured Pop had planned, make nice for the year I was supposed to live here, and give her a cut of the money." Dane didn't feel good confessing any of that—it was no wonder Suzy wasn't jumping into his arms for romance now.

"What million dollars?" Jack demanded.

"I don't think you ever got a letter," Dane said slowly, "I know Gabriel did. Pete did, too."

"What letter?" Jack asked impatiently. "I just read you the only letter I've received from Pop since that night."

Dane didn't have to ask what night. "The letter asking each of us to live here for a year, be a family. At the end of the year, each of us gets a million dollars."

Jack's eyes went wide. "And you still don't think this is a goodbye letter from a dying man? That order right there should have rung some warning bells for you. The prodigal father suddenly wants to be The Waltons? Wants the family to reunite? How was that supposed to happen? Over home movie reels and popcorn?" Jack snorted. "A million dollars doesn't buy love."

Dane thought that was probably true. Certainly it hadn't brought him closer to his brothers, his father or Suzy. "I was willing to go along with it because I needed the money."

"Everyone needs money, Dane. You think I ever win at rodeo?" Jack's eyes went hard and flat.

"Don't you?"

"Hell, no. Once, a long time ago, I won a small rodeo in a remote town up north. Can't even remember where I was. This was years ago. It paid out a couple of dinner tickets, a pair of boots and a hundred bucks, along with my entry fee. I don't have a truck. I pay for health insurance with what little place money I win. Believe me, just covering the health insurance as a rider is no picnic. I understand needing money. But I wouldn't be an indentured servant to Pop for it."

"*That's* what was bothering me. I didn't want to be indentured."

Jack jabbed a finger into Dane's chest. "Don't get married. You get roped twice."

Dane shook his head. "It was the money that bothered me, not the marriage. So what do you do all the time if you don't win? Why do you do it?"

Jack shrugged. "I like rodeo. It's my home. All my friends are there, like family. They *are* my family. I can count on them to give me a hitch to the next place, be there for me when I have a bad ride. It's hard to explain, but even if I don't win, I feel I'm still winning in life being around the rodeo. I see the country. And I don't owe anybody a thing."

"Okay. Still, here you are." Dane thought there had to be a reason his brother had shown up at the ranch.

"Because of this letter." Jack waved it in the air. "Pop's trying to put the curse of guilt on me."

"So tear it up."

"It's not that easy," Jack said. "The blessing of the father is very important. Was all through the Bible. Pop's never blessed me. Or any of us. But the past has to stay in the past in order for us to live our lives. We can't go back," he told Dane, his expression sincere. "You've heard the old expression, 'You can't go home'?"

"We don't want to go back," Dane pointed out. "What will it take for you to turn this letter into good karma? So that you can go on with your life and ride off into the sunset on a mean bounty bull?"

"I don't have to do anything because you're in the best position to turn the karma around. It's your wedding," Jack said. "Therefore, fortune is smiling on you. You have to find out what's wrong with Pop and fix it. Otherwise we'll never be free of him. I know you think I've been bucked off one too many times, but the old man's setting us up for being ruled from the grave."

Dane swallowed. "Maybe whatever it is can't be fixed."

Jack looked at his letter again. "He was never proud of me. That's what's so strange about this whole thing."

There was no arguing with that. Pop had hated the one thing Jack loved.

"He's dying," Jack said. "Or he wouldn't be looking for redemption, which he isn't getting from me. Forgiveness isn't something I'll be giving him on his deathbed." He gave Dane a mirthless smile. "You see why I know this is bad karma. We're supposed to honor our parents."

"Oh, hell," Dane murmured, "I called him the other day, and he's the same cold, remote person he always was. If you want this karma thing off your chest, call him and tell him you got his letter but not to bother in the future. It's not like he's found you a bride or anything. Or even tried to lure you home like he did the rest of us."

Jack stood. "You need to find out what the problem is. It'll bug you until you do."

"Thanks," Dane said. "Anyway, any problem Pop has, I can't solve."

"But at least," Jack said, "you can make the effort to let him know three-quarters of the family cares. Everybody wants to know their family cares, even gnarly old Pop. Best of luck with the wedding, even though I don't believe in getting married under the gun." Jack saluted him and slipped out the door.

"Heck," Dane muttered, "I do believe you've had your bell rung a few too many times, bro." Still, he couldn't help wondering if Jack cared a bit more than he was letting on.

Remembering that Jack had no vehicle, he glanced out the window to see if he could figure out how Jack had gotten to the ranch. He saw his brother hop into a waiting car. After a moment, the car pulled down the road. Dane stared, recognizing the vehicle even in the dark.

Suzy was giving his brother a ride away from the Morgan ranch.

"I TRIED TO TELL HIM," Jack told Suzy as they drove away. "But Dane is a man of facts. Comes from being a Ranger, probably. But I did try, just like you asked. Now tell me everything you know."

"I can't," Suzy said. "Patient confidentiality. Even though it's your father, I can't violate that."

"But you're not a nurse now," Jack pointed out.

"It doesn't matter."

"So you tell me Pop's not in good shape, and that's all?

How do I know you're not cooking up a scheme on Pop's behalf to get me jumping around like Gabriel and Dane?"

"Because," Suzy said carefully, "you didn't get a promise of a million dollars, or a handpicked bride with children, or anything that would make you feel like you had to do something you didn't want to."

"Do you think Dane's doing something he doesn't want to do?" Jack asked, his voice silky. "Like marry you?"

Suzy ignored that. She would wait and see how Dane felt about what Jack had told him before worrying about whether he'd change his mind about marrying her. "That's between Dane and me. All I wanted from you was the chance to let Dane know that he doesn't have forever to make amends with your father."

"Yeah, well. None of us care, little lady."

"And believe me, I appreciate that sentiment. I understand feeling betrayed by one's family. However, I know a different side of Mr. Morgan, and I...I don't want Dane to regret leaving things unsaid."

"He didn't seem too worked up about it." Jack shrugged and looked out the window. "Maybe he told you we're not a close family."

"Oh, quit carping about it," she snapped. "You're wearing it out like an old country tune. You have time to change the future, if not the past, if you want to."

"Did the old man tell you he was fond of disciplining us?" Jack asked. "His version of discipline was harsh, to put it mildly."

Suzy's skin chilled. "No. He didn't."

"He was harder on me than my brothers, I'll admit. And the last night we were all together, I'd barely gotten home from the hospital when Pop pitched the fit of all fits. I'd had it with him. I was tired of his insults and his griping and him trying to control my life. And I wasn't going to be 'disciplined' again." Jack's voice went tight with the memories. "This time, it was an all-out boxing match between us. If you think it's something to be proud of, fistfighting with your old man, you'd be wrong. I'd like to say I beat the old geezer fair and square, but he was always a tough old bird."

"And you were already injured," she murmured, wondering why Josiah couldn't have taken it easy on his son until another time when Jack was healed. But she knew why. He hated rodeo. He loved Jack. He wanted more out of life for his oldest son.

Still, Jack had basically nothing now. He owned his gear, by his own admission, and that was it.

"Yeah, I was injured, but I've never felt good about beating on the old man. Tough as rawhide and then some. He wore me down and then he let me know who was the head of the Morgan clan." Jack shook his head, grimacing. "I left as soon as I could pick myself up off the ground, and I'm not ever laying eyes on him again."

Suzy's fingers clenched on the steering wheel. "Dane never told me about that."

"Why should he? They left, too. No one wanted to be around the old man. Pete enlisted, Dane enlisted, Gabriel hitched around for a couple years and then enlisted. Whatever Pop was trying to make out of us, he failed miserably."

Tiny tears pricked at the back of Suzy's eyes. "I know it won't seem like much now, but I think he genuinely regrets that he wasn't a better father. He spends an awful lot of time with charity work and—"

"Lady, listen. Pop does what benefits Pop. Don't play the pity card with me, because I know him too well. If I was you, I'd concentrate on my wedding."

She caught her breath, hearing something in his voice. "How did Pete get the letter to you?"

"He left it at the rodeo, like I told you. A friend got it to me."

"And why did you decide to call me?"

"Because you'd told me you were marrying my brother. I called the house, hoping you'd answer the phone."

"But why?" Suzy asked. "I know what I wanted from you, but why did you call?"

Jack didn't speak for a while. Then he said, "The only wedding gift I can give you is my best wishes."

"Oh. Thank you." Suzy was touched, more than she could say. "Come if you can."

"I'll be in California by then, trying to ride off some of the guilt and bad karma Pop's trying to saddle me with. But I appreciate the invitation. By the way, my brothers mean a lot to me. I'd like to see them all married and happy, but not because Pop wants it." Jack got out of the car and grinned at her. "This is the end of the road for me."

"*Is* Dane happy?" she asked, dying to know. She knew Jack would be aware of his brother's true feelings.

"Don't you know?" Jack asked, his voice silky again.

"Not as much as you do about him."

"Then you better ask Dane," Jack said, "brother confidentiality and all that. Thanks for the ride—and thanks for trying to help us. Thing is, Morgan men are pretty set in their ways, if you hadn't already figured that out." With a wink, he shut the door and loped off into town.

Great. And I've fallen in love with a Morgan.

Chapter Seventeen

All the commotion at the Morgan ranch was a reminder to Suzy that she, too, had some past to clear up. So the next day she put Nicole and Sandra in the car and drove to Fort Wylie for what she knew would be an uncomfortable meeting. But she couldn't very well preach to the Morgan men about forgiving their father when she hadn't forgiven her own parents.

There was a lot on the line with this visit. If Dane hadn't shown the resolve to come out here and introduce himself to her father, maybe she wouldn't have considered it. The past was still too painful and raw. Yet as Dane said, there were Sandra and Nicole to consider. For them, Suzy would put aside her pride, lay her heart on the line one more time.

Until she did, she couldn't move on with her own life. The bad feelings—karma, Jack called it—would always be there, shackling her to yesterday. So she dressed her girls in their prettiest pink winter dresses and white tights and prayed time was the healer of all wounds.

At the gate, she pressed the intercom. The familiar voice of the housekeeper said, "Yes?"

"Mrs. Ross, it's Suzy."

"Suzy?" The housekeeper hesitated.

Suzy's pulse raced. Had Mrs. Ross been ordered not to allow her on the grounds? "Yes, ma'am," she replied.

The gate slid back without further hesitation. Suzy drove through, pained by the sight of the place where she'd once lived. Once upon a time, she'd dreamed of having children who would run and play on the wide lawns. Yet dreams didn't always come true.

Suzy parked her car by the steps, waving away the attendant who came to park it for her. "Thank you, John, we won't be staying long, I fear. How are you doing?"

He smiled at her, his gaze lighting with pleasure on her girls as she helped them from the car. "I'm fine. Keeping an eye on the old folks."

Suzy smiled. "Don't let them hear you call them that."

"Oh, I won't, don't you worry." He grinned at her.

Suzy went up the steps as the doors opened. "Hello, Mrs. Ross," she said as Sandra and Nicole took their time going up the marble steps, their little feet not quite sure on the smooth stone. Suzy held their hands to guide them.

"Hello, Suzy," Mrs. Ross replied. "And who might these young ladies be?"

"These are my daughters," Suzy said proudly. "This is Sandra, and this is Nicole." She pointed to each one in turn, pleased that Mrs. Ross seemed delighted to see the children.

"They look just like you, Suzy," Mrs. Ross said. "I've often wondered if they did. You know, when you were that age—"

Her voice trailed off as Suzy's parents appeared behind Mrs. Ross in the wide entryway.

"Hello, Mother. Father," Suzy said. Her girls clung to her legs, and Suzy thanked God for the strength they gave her.

"To what do we owe this visit?" her father asked.

Suzy straightened. "I wanted to tell you I'm getting married."

"So we heard," her father said. His gaze barely lit on his granddaughters, though her mother seemed to be studying them curiously. "Your cowboy friend was here the other night."

Mrs. Ross excused herself and surreptitiously left the entryway.

"My cowboy friend's name is Dane Morgan," Suzy said with a lift of her chin. "I didn't know he was coming out to introduce himself to you, but I'm happy he did."

Her father stared at her silently. Her mother seemed unwilling to say anything in case it might be the wrong thing. Sandra and Nicole stayed very still, sensing tension and not understanding it.

Forget this, Suzy thought suddenly, *if they don't want me and my children here, I've got a family elsewhere who does.*

"I seem to have come at a bad time," she said stiffly.

"If you'll excuse us, we should get back. I don't like to drive after dark."

And then, before she could react, Sandra went over and threw her arms around her grandfather's leg, just as she'd clung to Suzy. Nicole followed suit, not to be outdone, hugging his other leg. Their grandfather seemed puzzled by their action, then realized they were being affectionate, normal grandchildren. He raised his hands as if he didn't know what to do with them, and then he gently put a hand on each little girl's head, stroking their flyaway blond hair. This was the signal his wife seemed to be waiting for as she knelt down to touch each child for herself. After a moment of studying her gently lined face, Sandra and Nicole made their way into their grandmother's waiting arms. She hugged each grandchild to her tightly, kissing little round cheeks with joy. They patted her French knot of carefully brushed white hair with tiny toddler fingers, accepting the affection as if it were the most natural thing in the world, and Suzy was astonished to see tears running down her parents' faces.

THREE HOURS LATER, after a sumptuous meal of steak, red potatoes, asparagus and Oreo cake, Suzy allowed her parents to talk her into spending the night. For the sake of the children, they said, whom they wanted to spend more time with. They shouldn't be on the road so late, and Suzy had plenty of clothes at the house to wear.

Mrs. Ross sent for some nighties and essentials from her daughter who lived nearby and who had children about the same age. Suzy acquiesced, pleased that her parents wanted to spend more time with the twins.

She sat in her old room on her bed, with the children in a makeshift nursery in an adjoining room so she could hear them if they needed her in the night. Pulling out her cell phone, she called Cricket.

"Cricket, it's Suzy," she said.

"I know. Where are you? Dane's going nuts!"

"Why?" Suzy asked.

"Because he says you drove off with his brother Jack. And you haven't been home in hours, which is totally not like you. Dane thinks you're being enticed by Jack. Or something like that. Lured by danger."

"Lured by danger?" Suzy wrinkled her nose. "Have I ever been lured by danger?"

"Maybe he said you could be easily influenced to take a walk on the wild side. I can't remember exactly. I think he's jealous," she said in a hushed voice. "He's been stalking around here like a caged lion. He keeps saying it's time for the girls to be in bed or they'll get fussy."

Jealous didn't sound like Dane. "No, he's not jealous. Why would he think I was with Jack? I gave him a ride to town last night, and that was it. Jack was on his way to California, anyway."

"California?" Cricket repeated softly. "So he's not planning on being here for the wedding."

"No. He claims he has things to do."

"I see," Cricket murmured.

"So, back to Dane. Didn't you tell him I'd gone to my folks?"

"No. Priscilla and I both thought it might be best not to mention it. After all, he hadn't gotten the warmest reception there the other night—and it is your life, Suzy. We felt like if you'd wanted him to know, you would have told him. We're always going to be your friends first. If he'd gotten a little more wild, we probably would have had to say something, though. He said you wouldn't answer your cell phone, and a thousand crazy thoughts were going through his mind."

"I had it off. I just needed today to sort out my life." But she hadn't imagined Dane would have been so worried about her. "I'm staying at my parents' for the night. I'll call him later and tell him."

"Your parents?" Cricket's voice lit up. "Does that mean it was love at first sight when they saw those adorable little girls?"

Suzy smiled. "Although it was touch-and-go for a few minutes, the girls charmed them. And it was as if all the anger just dissolved. My parents act as if a miracle has happened."

"Oh, Suzy. I'm so happy for you!"

Suzy's eyes misted. "Thank you. I'm happier for my children. They deserve grandparents who love them." She'd wanted her parents' forgiveness more than she'd realized—she had dreamed of her children knowing their grandparents.

"Oh, it's like a fairy-tale ending," Cricket said. "I can't wait to tell Priscilla."

"What, what?" Suzy could hear Priscilla's voice as she came into the room.

"Just a minute and I'll tell you," Cricket said. "We've been touching up the last details for the wedding."

The wedding. She had forty-eight hours left. So little time to put her life into neat boxes. Hesitation filled her, a need for space and time to think. That was the real reason she'd accepted her parents' plea to stay with them. Everything in her life had suddenly changed. Her desire to never be without family—like Jack—had melted away without regret.

So now it was left to her to decide if she was making the right decision to marry Dane. She had to be honest with herself—it was time to go home for good.

Wherever home might be.

DANE WAS ABOUT TO GO OUT and hunt for Suzy. The idea that maybe she'd been in a car accident wreaked havoc with his good sense. Ever since he'd seen Suzy drive off with Jack, his gut felt as if a hole had been burned into it. The hole was deep and unfillable, and it screamed hunger. Insecurity. *Mine.*

Dane drew hard on his rational side, forcing himself to remember that brothers were brothers no matter how long they'd been separated. Family ties ran deeper than anything, although perhaps not Morgan ties. And maybe that's what was bothering him the most. He didn't feel secure in any way, not with Suzy, not with his family.

He sat down in the den in front of the TV, then decided the last thing he needed to do was fester. Putting on a jacket and gloves, he headed out to the barn to work off the strangest sensation that Suzy was slipping away from him.

SUZY WAS JUST ABOUT ASLEEP when she heard a soft knock on her door. "Suzy?" her mother said quietly. "Are you still awake?"

Suzy sat up. "Yes. Come in."

Her mother came in, wearing a deep-green velvet robe. She left the door a bit ajar, and Suzy turned on the lamp on her bedside table. For a moment her mother stood awkwardly at the foot of her bed, then settled on the edge as she'd done many times in Suzy's childhood.

"Suzy, your father and I have been talking."

Suzy waited, not knowing what to say.

"We want you to know we're sorry for the things we said to you. We've lost a lot of time, precious time, by being more concerned about our reputation than your welfare. I, especially, am to blame because I should have encouraged your father to bend. Frankly, we didn't know what to think, and we let our pride rule us." Her mother shook her head, wiped at her eyes. "I would give anything to turn back time and do it all over. Be a better mother to you. Know my grandchildren." She shook her head. "But I can't. All I can do now is ask your forgiveness."

"Oh, Mom," Suzy murmured. She basked in the emotional warmth she'd so badly missed. "Everything works out for the best."

"I'm not so sure." Her mother peered at her intently. "I'm afraid you're marrying this man because you feel you must. I'd just like to know that the lack of family support isn't making you do something you'll regret later. It's easier to cancel a wedding than get a divorce." She swallowed, nervously wringing her hands in her lap. "Not that I'm saying your intended didn't seem like a very nice man. But the mother in me would like to see you and my grandchildren have the very best you can, a marriage that you will treasure forever, a man who means to be a wonderful husband and father."

Suzy hesitated. Nothing about the short-term marriage she and Dane were planning fit her mother's description. The truth was—and Dane would agree— they weren't getting married for the right reasons at all.

"In the morning, your father and I would like to have a financial discussion with you." Her mother looked at her. "You are our only child, and your children are our only grandchildren. I realize we're asking a lot of you at the last minute, but we think it's best to have this conversation before your wedding."

Suzy looked into her mother's eyes, seeing regret and hope for the future. "It's going to be all right, Mom," she said, and her mother's eyes filled with tears again.

"I know," her mother finally said, trying for a brave

smile. "But only if you're getting married to this man with all your heart and soul. I just want you to be sure, because you'll always have a home right here."

Chapter Eighteen

In the morning, Suzy learned she was an heiress. The amount of money in trust for her alone would make her wealthy beyond her wildest imagination. What she would one day inherit was staggering. Never again would she know need. Her girls would never worry about where the next meal was coming from, how she would pay for their health insurance, or a thousand other worries that had haunted her.

Before Josiah Morgan's generous gift, she'd wondered how her children would ever go to college. It was almost surreal, Cinderella-like, to go to bed one night wondering about her children's future, and the next morning wake up and find that all her worries had been waved away like magic.

"You don't have to get married, unless you're truly marrying for love," her father said. "We want you to be happy."

She wasn't marrying for love. Dane did not love her. He might love her children, but he was not in love with their mother. They had talked about this being a short-term marriage. "Thank you, Mom, Dad," Suzy said. "To be honest, it means more to me that you want to be with my children."

They sat quietly together for a few moments thinking, Suzy knew, about all the harsh words that had been spoken. Maybe she wouldn't have thought about marrying Dane if she hadn't felt such a great need for a family connection; if she hadn't felt an enormous sense of gratitude to Josiah.

That all seemed very far away as she sat in the house she'd grown up in.

"Tell us how we can help you," her mother said. "I know there must be so many things going through your mind."

Suzy took a deep, bracing breath. "There is a lot to think about, but in the meantime, Dad, I need you to give me away tomorrow night."

Tears sprang into her father's eyes. "I already gave you away once, because of my stubbornness."

"That doesn't count," Suzy said quickly. "We're not ever going to think about that again. We're a family again, and that's all that matters."

"I don't know if I can give you away to a man I don't even know. I wish you'd take some more time to think about it." His tone was pleading. "Your mother and I believe that if this is the right thing for you, a little time won't make any difference."

That was true. But Suzy knew that when she'd had nothing, Josiah had been there. Josiah wanted his boys married, he wanted grandchildren—she could admit to herself now that the old man probably had schemed a grand matchmaking plot to get some of his sons to marry, carry on the family name while he was still alive to see it. She felt a special fondness for Josiah, rascal that he was, because she knew even the best families hit rough patches. Even before he'd gifted her children with college educations, she'd known he was a good man—she loved him like a father. She knew he was sick.

Some gifts weren't monetary. "I'm going to marry Dane," she said softly. "For him, for my daughters and for me, I think it's a good match."

Her father nodded. Her mother wiped away some tears with a lace hankie, though she tried to smile. "I'm sure you've given great consideration to your marriage," her mother said. "We support your decision and know you've chosen a man who will be a good father to your girls. I'm pretty sure that's what's driving you now, Suzy, and I completely understand."

"Thank you." Nicole and Sandra and Josiah—there were so many reasons Suzy knew she would say *I do* at the altar tomorrow night.

"In the meantime," her father said, clearing his throat, "could we invite your fiancé out here for a spur-of-the-moment luncheon?"

Suzy looked at him. "I'm sure Dane would be glad to come out, but is there something more than the usual welcome to the family greeting on your mind?"

"In light of your financial situation," her father said,

"we think it's best to ask Dane to sign a prenuptial agreement. I'm sure you understand why we feel this way. No matter whom you marry, we would advise that in the interest of estate and succession planning. There's simply a lot at stake, and it's our responsibility to secure your future, and that of the children."

Suzy blinked. "You want Dane to come out here to sign some papers? Meet with lawyers the day he marries me?"

"Suzy, we didn't have a lot of notice," her mother reminded her. "It's not about Dane, it's about your security, and the twins' future."

"I understand," Suzy said slowly, thinking that Josiah of all people would understand the necessity of legal documents. "But it's a very difficult thing to spring on someone right before their wedding."

"I should think that if he really loves you, he'll understand our desire to protect you," her father said.

Dane would sign the papers without complaint—she just didn't want to ask him to be so cold and business-like about their future. She wanted…romance? Mystery? The feeling of me-and-you-against-the-world? Why did this request of her parents seem so cold and calculated?

The past haunted her. She'd had one man leave her without looking back as soon as he'd learned she would have no part of her family's fortune. Yet Dane was not a man to whom money mattered greatly—he had none, he said he wouldn't take his father's money for marrying her. So why was she bothered by a practical request?

Their "simple" marriage plan was getting complicated. In fact, it had begun to get more involved as soon as they'd applied for the marriage license. Josiah had plans, her parents, her friends—everybody wanted to act in the interest of their marriage. She supposed she was being irresponsible to not appreciate the many facets of joining two people together—but marrying Dane at one time had seemed more like an adventure than a business plan. "I'll invite him," she said slowly, "but not for an afternoon of lawyers and documents. I want you two to just spend time with him and get to know him."

"You need more time to think," her mother said.

To that, Suzy simply said, "Yes."

"It's a lot. It can be overwhelming, I know," her mother replied. "Your young man is taking on a lot of responsibility for you, which I admire."

Dane was getting a wife, two children and legal documents. It was a lot, for a man who wanted to spend his life parasailing in Mexico.

Why was he doing it?

DANE HANDED MRS. ROSS A BOUQUET of flowers when she opened the door to let him in.

"Thank you," she said, surprised. "For the lady of the house?"

"No, for you," Dane said. "It's a bribe so that you'll always open the gate for me whenever I'm in town."

Mrs. Ross smiled. "I work at the behest of my employers, but if it were up to me, you would get the code to the gate."

"Excellent. One convert to my charm. Show me in to the ice room," he said.

Dane could see Mrs. Ross was fighting against it, but he saw her smile before she went back to being her formal self. "Please follow me."

She escorted him into the white room where Suzy's parents, Suzy and the two girls waited. Dane grinned as the little girls ran unevenly to throw their arms around his legs. "Hello, baby dolls! Have you missed me?" He stood, holding his hand out for the Winterstones. This time, Dr. Winterstone shook his hand, and Mrs. Winterstone smiled at him. Dane felt as if he was making rapid progress.

"Thank you for coming out," Dr. Winterstone said.

Mrs. Winterstone added, "Especially on such short notice."

Dane smiled at Suzy, reassured now that he saw she was fine. She looked pretty, if a little worried, which bothered him, but he figured she was nervous about her big day. What bride wouldn't be? He had a few butterflies himself. He was just glad she seemed to have worked things out with her parents. It boded well for their future.

"We're sorry to have to ask you out here on business matters," Dr. Winterstone said, "but I'm sure you appreciate the importance of—"

"Dad," Suzy said. "Could I have a moment alone with Dane, please?"

"Certainly, Suzy," her mother said. "Why don't you take Dane into the library? We'll watch Nicole and Sandra."

Dane's sense of apprehension grew as he was walked into a massive library, with floor-to-ceiling shelves of books arranged in dark paneling. Flowing curtains tumbled gracefully down the casements of long windows; expensive artwork graced the walls. "Wow," he said, "just like a presidential library."

Suzy didn't smile. "Dane, my parents' invitation today wasn't just about lunch and getting to know you before the wedding."

He smiled at her. "Your father has agreed to give us his blessing? Tell me I can have your hand in marriage? Whatever it is, smile, Suzy. We've survived a lot of family interference up till now."

"I know," she said, "but this is a bit different."

He leaned against a very senatorial-looking writing desk and pulled her toward him. "So shoot."

"My parents would like for you to sign a prenuptial agreement."

That caught him by surprise. "Sign a prenuptial agreement? For what purpose?"

"It will say that everything I have before the wedding remains mine…should we divorce. And of course, we are divorcing, although I didn't tell them that, so it does make sense to legally—"

He held up his hand. "Suzy, I don't want anything of yours. I want you and the girls. Is that going to be in the agreement, or do I have to sign off rights for that, too?"

"No, of course not," Suzy said, pulling slightly away from him, distancing herself, and suddenly, Dane realized what he was really up against. It wasn't so much the legalese; it was the specter of divorce a year from now that had Suzy tightening up on him. Almost freezing him out with her face turned from him. Body language that said *I have to protect myself.*

"Suzy," he said, "I don't know what to say. I'll sign the damn papers, I don't care, although I think my word alone should suffice. I don't even want the money my father would give me for living in his house for a year. If I want money, I'd like back what I lost to my partner." He let her go because he sensed she needed space and Suzy sat down in an oversize leather chair, looking defenseless.

"Dane, what are we doing?" she asked.

He shook his head. At that moment, he wasn't certain anymore.

AFTER THE LAWYERS arrived—two of them—and every paper had been signed, Dane and Suzy's entire marriage had been wrapped in businesslike terms. Although he'd proposed a formal merger to Suzy in the first place, he'd certainly learned today what a real business transaction was.

Stiffly, he extended a hand to Dr. and Mrs. Winterstone. "I'll be on my way, then."

"You won't stay for tea?" Mrs. Winterstone asked.

Dane shook his head. "We're having fried chicken and ribs from the Trusty Bucket at our rehearsal dinner. Suzy and I would love to introduce you to our friends and my family, what little family is in town."

Mrs. Winterstone shook her head. "Thank you, but we must decline. Suzy, may we keep the girls for the night? You must have an awful lot to do for tomorrow."

Dane let out a long breath he'd been holding in, glad to hear her parents ask about Nicole and Sandra. The girls deserved family who adored them as much as he did.

"They'd love that. Dane, I'll be back at the ranch soon." Suzy barely met his gaze as Mrs. Winterstone walked him to the door.

"Thank you again for coming by," Mrs. Winterstone said. "We will, of course, be at the wedding tomorrow night."

Dane inclined his head, not sure what to say to this woman who would now be his mother-in-law. Shouldn't he hug her? Kiss her cheek? What did one do when called out to sign off on prenuptial documents? "It's a very informal wedding," he finally said.

To her credit, Mrs. Winterstone didn't wince. "I'm sure it will be lovely. Dr. Winterstone and I will give you two our wedding gift then."

She smiled, a little wobbly, and Dane realized how hard it was for her to give away her only child when she'd just gotten her back. Swiftly, he leaned down to gently hug her. "I'm going to take good care of her," he said.

Mrs. Winterstone added, "If she'll let you," and they

both laughed a little so that Dane felt better as she closed the double doors behind him.

Then he realized Suzy hadn't walked with him to say goodbye and didn't feel better at all.

"You're leaving, sir?" John asked. "May I get your vehicle for you this time? If you're going to be part of the family, I should acquaint myself with it. My employers won't be happy if I'm not doing my job."

Dane glanced back toward the house and handed John the keys. "I'll be here often. And when you see Miss Winterstone-soon-to-be-Morgan, will you please tell her I'll get my goodbye kiss from her later?"

The attendant grinned as he jogged to get Dane's truck. "Will do, sir," he called over his shoulder.

Dane whistled to himself, biding his time, knowing that soon, he'd be kissing Suzy Winterstone at the altar.

She would be all his.

Chapter Nineteen

Dane returned to the Morgan ranch first, finding Cricket and Priscilla in the kitchen in a mad rush to finish the cakes. "Your father ordered more," Cricket told him.

"Why didn't you just order them from Valentine's bakery in town?" Dane asked. The women were working up a storm, and he wondered if his father knew how much effort the ladies were putting into their creations.

"Because your father is paying us," Priscilla revealed. "Enough to make us think we should go into the catering business. Seriously. And it beats making drapes."

He dipped his finger into a mixing bowl, tasting the frosting with appreciation. "Maybe you *should* open a catering business. This is tasty stuff. I know a certain bride and groom who are very lucky to have such good friends."

The ladies smiled at him. "For a first-time effort, we feel pretty good," Cricket told him. "By the way, how did it go with the Winterstones?" Her tone sounded as if she didn't expect much from that meeting.

Dane shrugged. "They were very nice. Suzy seemed

tense, but she frequently does." He grinned. "I have her to myself tonight, however, and I intend to loosen her up."

Cricket and Priscilla glanced at each other. "Where are the girls?" Priscilla asked.

"Suzy's parents are keeping them so we can attend the rehearsal dinner." Dane smiled his most charming, the-devil-made-me-do-it grin. "They couldn't have given me a better wedding gift than a night with my bride-to-be."

"That's wonderful," Cricket said, looking at Priscilla, "because we had planned to stay at Suzy's cottage for the night so you two could be alone."

The two of them were up to their elbows in flour and sugar and didn't look as if they'd planned to leave the kitchen anytime soon. "This is a lot of cake."

"We decided we wanted to make some desserts to go with the food tonight," Priscilla explained. "It's a big occasion, you know."

"It's a rehearsal dinner," Dane said. "Who will be here besides the family and you two? Gabriel and Laura, me, Suzy, you two…that should do it? Right?"

"Pastor Riley," Cricket said. "Suzy decided she wanted me to be co-maid of honor with Priscilla since there will be so many guests. We needed extra ushers, too, so Gabriel asked Mason Jefferson to press a few of his brothers into service. And I think your father may have invited a few close friends," Cricket said. "We're planning to feed fifty tonight."

"Fifty!" Dane could see his quiet evening romancing Suzy slipping away. "Why?"

"So many people are helping out," Cricket explained. "Turns out folks are donating food, tables, chairs and so on. Your father said he felt like he couldn't leave anybody out of the biggest wedding of the year."

Dane blinked. "It was supposed to be a small, subdued affair."

"Well, your father instructed us to spare no expense. He said he also planned to toast Laura and Gabriel since he didn't get to give them a wedding. To be honest, I think your pop is simply in a celebratory mood," Cricket told him. She beamed, as if it was the most natural thing in the world for a man's wedding to be orchestrated by a renegade father and well-meaning friends.

"When did he tell you this?" Dane demanded, and Priscilla smiled.

"All week long. He's been on the phone like it's a hotline, giving us instructions and checking on our progress." Cricket patted his arm. "You would have noticed except you've been busy with other things."

He sat down and snagged a tiny cake off a platter. "Mmm. What is this?"

"A petit four." Priscilla tapped his hand with a wooden spoon to discourage more snitching. "They're for a party Laura is giving Suzy tonight, after the rehearsal dinner. Laura's friend Mimi Jefferson dropped them off from Valentine's." A teasing smile touched Priscilla's face. "Hope you didn't have plans for tonight that included Suzy, because we're giving her a little surprise lingerie shower."

He could feel his mood, which had been slipping downward as he learned of all the special events, lighten considerably. "Well, if it's lingerie, I can certainly wait my turn for Suzy's limited time." He tried to sound angelic but failed miserably, judging by Cricket's and Priscilla's laughter. "What? Every guy likes to know that his bride will have lacy stuff." He shrugged. "Not gonna lie about that."

The front door opened and Suzy came in, stopping when she saw the usually tidy kitchen in disarray. "What have I gotten you two into?" she asked, hugging them both. "Have you been in here all day?" She glanced at Dane over their shoulders, her eyes huge. He grinned at her, knowing she was going to go into panic mode.

He'd felt the same when he'd seen all the hard work on their behalf, and then realized that was what he'd been missing in his life—friends and family who were always there. "Working like bridesmaids," he said.

"Except bridesmaids usually don't have to do anything more than hold the bride up and keep her from running off." Suzy looked at Dane, and she did appear to be a little nervous, as he'd expected.

"Oh, you're not going anywhere," he said, sweeping her into his arms. "You're home for good now."

Suzy went upstairs to the room she was used to sharing with the girls, feeling empty and alone without Nicole and Sandra. Downstairs, she heard the front door slam as Priscilla and Cricket left for her house to get ready for the rehearsal dinner. They'd decided they would move into her little place, commandeering it for themselves so they'd have a quiet place away from all the festivities. Suzy thought that was a great idea because she didn't live that far away, and her home, though small, was comfortable and private.

She was aware that her friends were trying to give her some space to be alone with Dane. The thought made her so nervous she didn't know what to do. Slowly, she dressed for the evening, wondering if it was necessary to rehearse something that was so short-term. The whole wedding had grown into a huge, elaborate affair more suited to people who planned to be married for a lifetime together. She felt ashamed, as if she was duping her friends.

It was all because of Josiah and his sky-high plans, and Suzy knew he would grin if he knew he was making her feel guilty. She wondered if Dane felt the same.

A knock on the door made her jump. "Yes?"

"It's Dane, Suzy. Can I talk to you for a minute?"

She drew a deep breath. A minute…a year…a lifetime—she could hardly say no. It was the last word she could think of that she would ever want to say to him.

She opened the door. "Please come in."

He looked so handsome in a charcoal blazer and blue jeans, black felt cowboy hat and a confident smile. His gaze slid over the long blue evening dress Priscilla had lent her. It was very slinky, yet demure. She'd loved it the moment she'd seen it.

"Sexy," he said, and Suzy could feel herself blush.

"Not sexy," she murmured.

"Oh, yeah," he said. "Sexy."

Were her ankles trembling? She was a full-grown woman with children—there was no reason she should be so jumpy around this man. "So you wanted to talk about…?"

"About tonight. And tomorrow. And the year."

She looked at him, waiting.

"So you're all good with your visit to your parents?"

Her smile was sure. "I feel free. Free of the past."

The new life with her family was a miracle she hadn't anticipated. The joy of it still washed over her. Yet she felt bad for the prenup incident and wondered if that was what he wanted to discuss. "I didn't tell my folks we were only marrying for a year. I didn't know they would ask you to sign a prenuptial agreement."

He touched a finger to her chin, lifting it so he could see her eyes. "I know that. They were only looking out for your best interests, and the children's, no less than I would in the same situation."

"Thank you," she murmured. "Part of me thought you'd understand, but it was so awkward. You hadn't asked me to sign anything."

"That's because I have nothing." He grinned, and if it was true he had nothing, he was the sexiest poor man she'd ever seen. "All I want you to sign is the marriage certificate."

"I'm going to sign that."

"Good." His palm took the place of his finger on her

chin, sliding along her face and then cupping the back of her neck. "I'm looking forward to seeing your name as Suzy Morgan."

"Dane, do you feel like this wedding got out of hand?"

"Yes," he said, "I do feel that way. I've felt that way for some time. Everything has gotten way out of hand, especially my feelings for you." And then he kissed her, making her heart beat hard, sending her blood running through her like sizzling lightning. He kissed her harder, stole her breath, and Suzy felt herself collapsing into his strength, wanting more of him. Holding him tightly to her, she responded to his kisses, the fire of his passion warming her, then scorching her like nothing she'd ever known.

He eased her back onto the bed, trying to be gentle, careful of the gown she wore, but Suzy pulled him forward, dragging him with her, knowing that the beautiful gown was in the way of what she wanted. "Hang on," she said. "I can't reach the zipper."

"I can. Don't worry about that." The zipper went, the dress flew, the heels dropped to the floor, and Dane had never undressed himself more quickly.

A moment later, he lay wrapped in Suzy's arms, and the feel of her underneath him, the soft, silkiness of her against his body blew his mind. "Are you okay with this?" he asked. "I want you to be—"

Suzy pulled him down to kiss her. "I want you, too. Now make love to me, because this is one last thing I have to know before I marry you."

He said, "What one last thing?" before remembering her startling confession, and then he laughed.

"Suzy," he said, "from this day forward, you're a different woman. If you're still worried about being bad in bed, rest assured I expect you to be very bad in my bed." Gently he kissed her lips, taking his time with her mouth, stroking inside her, intending to take forever, but then his little bride-to-be surprised him by rolling him over and getting on top.

"You're too slow," she said.

"Then hang on," Dane said, as he grabbed hold of her sassy bottom, rocking inside her and the next thing he knew, Suzy had forgotten all about whatever had been worrying her as she cried out his name.

That's when he had to face the truth—he didn't want just one year with Suzy Winterstone.

He wanted forever.

Chapter Twenty

Dane was living large, and he knew it. He'd fallen under Suzy's spell, which was a wonderful thing. The woman had made love to him before the rehearsal dinner, then in the upstairs bathroom when she'd told him she needed help "powdering her nose and making sure her zipper wasn't stuck," and—glory be—she'd spent the entire night in his bed, modeling one after another of her new lingerie from the bridal shower.

He was exhausted. And the happiest man on the earth. He wasn't certain he could keep up with his bride-to-be, however, if she was going to be this insatiable.

Glancing out the window, he could see guests milling about on the grounds. Tables were set up, bows on chairs blew softly in the breeze. The table and chairs he'd made for Sandra and Nicole were adorned with ribbons to match the adult tables, perfect for tiny girls. It was a balmy sixty-eight degrees with the sun shining so most people only wore light coats. He wondered if they should have had the ceremony at the church, but

Suzy had said that the Morgan ranch was where Josiah would want it to be, and he'd acquiesced with some misgivings. It seemed they did enough for Josiah's sake, and the old man wasn't even here, Dane thought, a bit annoyed. Surely he was going to attend the wedding, see that his son had finally done something to make him proud.

That's when he knew Suzy was right—he still wanted Pop's approval. It wasn't why he was marrying Suzy, but he wanted his father there. What had started out as a sham, a marriage to pacify his father, had turned into a full-blown desire to be married and a wish that Pop could witness him making good at the only thing that he'd learned really mattered in life—being a family man.

It didn't look like Pop planned to attend the very shindig he'd taken such an active hand in directing. Yet that was Pop—totally unpredictable. Dane told himself he wasn't disappointed. In thirty minutes, he'd be a husband, a father and a son-in-law. Now all that was left was the *Til death do us part*.

How he was going to talk Suzy into that, he still hadn't figured out. Now that he'd made love to her, he knew he was never letting her go. She was the best thing that had ever happened to him. If Pop had picked Suzy for Dane, then he'd known exactly what he was doing.

"It's time," Gabriel said, coming into the room where Dane stared down at the guests. "Time to turn in your ticket to Mexico."

Dane laughed. "That seems like such a crazy plan now."

Gabriel brushed off the shoulders of Dane's black suit jacket, checking for wrinkles. "That's the bachelor way. Everything seems possible. Then you get married."

"And then?" Dane asked, looking at his brother.

Gabriel smiled. "And then you realize that there are some things in life that are even better than living in Mexico."

"Good to know." Dane had already figured that out, however. "I thought Pop might make it into town. He organized all this, with some willing accomplices."

Gabriel shrugged. "You know Pop. He'll always be footloose."

"Yeah." Dane took a deep breath. "Ever hear from Pete?"

"No. He'll be back. In his own time, of course. Jack, too."

"You think?" Dane found that hard to believe of Jack.

"Sure. One day."

Dane didn't think so. Jack would have to be hog-tied and dragged back. "You ever think it was strange Pop set his matchmaking skills on you and me, but not Pete and Jack?"

"No," Gabriel said. "As Pop used to say, Pete was his James Bond and Jack his James Dean. Either of those guys ever settle down?"

Dane shook his head. "No."

"Well, then." Gabriel grinned as he watched more guests arrive. "I think half the town is here."

"More than that. Pop always had to be over-the-top."

"He'd love this," Gabriel said. "He loves being the center of attention."

"So when did you know it was forever with you and Laura?"

"When I first saw her," Gabriel said, "although I didn't realize it at the time. I just didn't want Pop running my life, so I fought it like mad. In the end, I didn't care anymore how I found Laura, whether it was because Pop wanted me to or the good Lord had made it happen. All that mattered was Penny and Perrin at the time."

That explained perfectly how Dane felt. "Suzy could have had any man. She chose me."

Gabriel gave him a slap on the back. "Don't screw it up, then."

Dane snorted. "I won't."

"Come on. Let's go find your bride."

Dane followed his brother out. Nearby, friends played romantic wedding music, very churchlike and proper. Elegant. He saw a black limousine pull up, and John the driver assisting Dr. Winterstone from the car. Mrs. Ross helped Mrs. Winterstone out. The little girls hopped out, running across the grass when they saw him. He swung each of them into his arms. "Hello! Are these my little flower girls?"

Dr. and Mrs. Winterstone walked over, attired in less-than-formal wear, he noticed with some relief. She had on a pretty pear-green suit, and he wore a charcoal-gray suit. More importantly, they both wore big smiles on their faces. "Glad you could make it," Dane said with a grin.

"We wouldn't miss our daughter's wedding for the world," replied Mrs. Winterstone.

Dr. Winterstone glanced around. "This is a nice place."

"Thanks," Dane said. "It's Pop's. He's not here right now, but if he makes it to the wedding, I'll make sure you meet him."

Dr. Winterstone looked at him. "*If* he makes it?"

"Did I mention he lives in France?" Dane asked with a smile. "Pop is sort of a world-traveler."

"Ah, yes," Dr. Winterstone said. "Which reminds me, we'd like to present you with a wedding gift. How would you feel about first-class tickets and accommodations to Paris for a weeklong honeymoon? We would, of course, be more than happy to watch Sandra and Nicole, the darling namesakes of my wife, Sandra Nicole." He and Mrs. Winterstone smiled proudly.

Dane grinned. Clearly their chief goal was spending time with their grandchildren. "I have a feeling Suzy would love that."

"All right, Mother. Let's go get a seat," Dr. Winterstone said. "Do we have to wait for an usher to seat us, or do we just pick a chair?" He glanced at the hundred folding chairs uncertainly.

"You just go choose a chair near the front," Dane told him, "your services will be required to give away the bride."

"That's right," Dr. Winterstone said, perking up. "I guess I'll do that." He ran a quick eye over Dane, then nodded.

Dane grinned. "I'll have my turn one day."

Dr. Winterstone smiled. "I'm just glad to have my daughter back. Don't really feel like I'm giving her away at all, so I have you to thank for that."

Dane gave him a gentle pat on the back. "Take a seat and enjoy the day. We're all going to be eating cake soon enough, if I can find my bride."

At that moment, a bridal march began to play softly. Dane turned, seeing the co-maids of honor, Cricket and Priscilla, walking down the porch, followed by his bride-to-be, looking like a vision out of a fairy tale. Dane's breath caught. "Look at your mother," he told the little girls who clung to his legs, "one day you'll look just like her."

Gabriel tapped him on the shoulder. "Let me walk you up to the altar, bro. Pretty sure that's where you're supposed to be, if you want to get married."

"And I do. Come on, girls."

They followed Dane in their pretty white dresses overlaid with tulle and lace, wearing white gloves and matching knit sweaters for warmth. The guests chuckled and smiled as the girls passed by, shy with all the people sitting in the chairs watching. Dane took his place at the altar, and Dr. Winterstone went to give his arm to his daughter as she walked down the white runner aisle between the chairs. As Suzy walked toward him, Dane knew he was the luckiest man on earth. With his girls standing beside him, and Suzy's hand in his, Dane promised to love and cherish Suzy forever.

Then he leaned to whisper something in her ear—very out of the ordinary Priscilla would have said—but whatever it was, it seemed to make Suzy joyfully happy, because instead of just one kiss to seal the deal, she threw her arms around her husband's neck and kissed him as if she was the happiest bride on earth, one who knew she was going to be married to her man for much, much longer than three hundred and sixty-five days.

And then as he hugged Suzy and his girls to him, Dane glimpsed his father on horseback, silhouetted against the horizon, close enough to see his big grin as he proudly waved his cowboy hat in celebration.

Please join Dr. and Mrs. Winterstone and
Suzy Winterstone Morgan
on February 1
for a light reception to honor
Sandra and Nicole Winterstone Morgan
the proud daughters of their new father, Dane Morgan
God has blessed our family in so many ways

* * * * *

Despite his protestations, Pete returns to the Morgan ranch to confront his father, and what he finds there completely takes him by surprise!

Turn the page for a sneak peek at Pete's story,
THE SECRET AGENT'S SURPRISES,
coming in February 2009,
only from Harlequin American Romance.

Chapter One

Pete Morgan sat in a bar in Riga, Latvia, tired, cold and inwardly annoyed as he remembered the letter he'd received from his father, Josiah, in January. The missive was a parting shot, designed to make him feel guilty. Wasn't the pen supposed to be mightier than the sword? The letter hadn't had the desired effect—it had only ignited old feelings of resentment. He wouldn't admit to a saint that he'd been steaming since the two letters had been found in a kitchen drawer at the Morgan ranch, one for him and one for his oldest brother, Jack. Pete had left that letter for Jack with a rodeo manager, knowing it would reach Jack eventually.

Now it was February, and the memory of his father's words still set his teeth on edge. He knew every word by heart:

Dear Pete,
Of all my sons, you were the most difficult. I saw

in you an unfulfilled version of myself, a man who would never be able to settle. I write this letter knowing that you will never live at the Morgan ranch attempting to be part of the family again. Like Jack, you hold long grudges. If by the time I pass away, you have not lived at the ranch for the full year, your million dollars will be split among the brothers who have fulfilled their family obligation.
Pop

It was a kick in the teeth, not so much because of the money but because his father lacked trust in him, basic faith that he cared about his own family. Wasn't it Pop's fault that no one cared to be at the ranch or have any contact with him? To receive this missive out of the blue had sent Pete packing to the other side of the world, although he'd been seriously considering retiring from the world of espionage.

Jack's letter—which he'd read—had been worse:

Jack,
I tried to be a good father. I tried to save you from yourself. In the end, I realized that you are too different from me. But I was always proud of my firstborn son.

This was Pop, always playing the brothers off each other, which was how the trouble had begun so many years ago, driving a wedge between them that still existed today, at least for two of them.

The other two, Gabriel and Dane, had made up with the old man. They'd married, had children. Collected their million.

But now the stakes were higher. Pop had come home to live at the Morgan ranch to enjoy the grandchildren and new family he'd netted with all his matchmaking and machinations.

If Pop thought Pete had any intention of living under the same roof with him, he was mistaken. Pete would sit freezing in the darkest side of hell before that happened.

No woman, no family, no million dollars, would ever tie him to the ornery son of a gun who was his father— Pop had foretold the future ominously.

Pete would never settle down. He did indeed hold long grudges—he'd learned it from the master, Josiah Morgan.

There was something satisfying in being the blackest sheep a man could be.

'I've found her.'

Max froze.

It was what he'd been waiting for since June, but now—now he was almost afraid to voice the question. His heart stalling, he leaned slowly back in his chair and scoured the investigator's face for clues. 'Where?' he asked, and his voice sounded rough and unused, like a rusty hinge.

'In Suffolk. She's living in a cottage.'

Living. His heart crashed back to life, and he sucked in a long, slow breath. All these months he'd feared—

'Is she well?'

'Yes, she's well.'

He had to force himself to ask the next question. 'Alone?'

The man paused. 'No. The cottage belongs to a man called John Blake. He's working away at the moment, but he comes and goes.'

God. He felt sick. So sick he hardly registered the

next few words, but then gradually they sank in. 'She's got *what?*'

'Babies. Twin girls. They're eight months old.'

'Eight—?' he echoed under his breath. 'They must be his.'

He was thinking out loud, but the P.I. heard and corrected him.

'Apparently not. I gather they're hers. She's been there since mid-January last year, and they were born during the summer—June, the woman in the post office thought. She was more than helpful. I think there's been a certain amount of speculation about their relationship.'

He'd just bet there had. God, he was going to kill her. Or Blake. Maybe both of them.

'Of course, looking at the dates, she was presumably pregnant when she left you, so they could be yours, or she could have been having an affair with this Blake character before…'

He glared at the unfortunate P.I. 'Just stick to your job. I can do the math,' he snapped, swallowing the unpalatable possibility that she'd been unfaithful to him before she'd left. 'Where is she? I want the address.'

'It's all in here,' the man said, sliding a large envelope across the desk to him. 'With my invoice.'

'I'll get it seen to. Thank you.'

'If there's anything else you need, Mr Gallagher, any further information—'

'I'll be in touch.'

'The woman in the post office told me Blake was

away at the moment, if that helps,' he added quietly, and opened the door.

Max stared down at the envelope, hardly daring to open it, but when the door clicked softly shut behind the P.I., he eased up the flap, tipped it and felt his breath jam in his throat as the photos spilled out over the desk.

Oh, lord, she looked gorgeous. Different, though. It took him a moment to recognise her, because she'd grown her hair, and it was tied back in a ponytail, making her look younger and somehow freer. The blond highlights were gone, and it was back to its natural soft golden-brown, with a little curl in the end of the ponytail that he wanted to thread his finger through and tug, just gently, to draw her back to him.

Crazy. She'd put on a little weight, but it suited her. She looked well and happy and beautiful, but oddly, considering how desperate he'd been for news of her for the past year—one year, three weeks and two days, to be exact—it wasn't only Julia who held his attention after the initial shock. It was the babies sitting side by side in a supermarket trolley. Two identical and absolutely beautiful little girls.

* * * * *

When Max Gallagher hires a P.I. to find his estranged wife, Julia, he discovers she's not alone—she has twin baby girls, and they might be his. Now workaholic Max has just two weeks to prove that he can be a wonderful husband and father to the family he wants to treasure.

Look for TWO LITTLE MIRACLES
by Caroline Anderson,
available February 2009
from Harlequin Romance®.